THE OCTOPUS AT THE VATICAN

THE OCTOPUS AT THE VATICAN

Christophe Mercier

Although inspired by real characters and historical facts, this story is fiction. Scenes including historic people are pure falsehood and do not represent reality.

The mythological Chimera spits fire.
She has three heads of a snake of a goat and of a lion.

DEDICATION

to my wonderful family and friends

THE FIRE

March—May 1978

May 12, 1978 - Cinisi (Sicily)

Alessa Lombardi was alone among the olive trees in the valley. The river was dry. The town of Cinisi stood in front of her. Behind her, the vale narrowed to a steep slope, she had just left. On the right, the hillside was sharp, like the olive groves in Corfu where she spent holidays with her parents as a child. To the left, the hillock was softer.

The local election had taken place the week before, with an odd outcome. Peppino Impastato had been elected when everyone knew he had just been murdered. The popular message to Cosa Nostra was clear.

Alessa took a few photos to remember the site for her articles. According to what she had been told in town, this must be the place Peppino Impastato's father had been killed a year earlier.

"Not a place for a murder, she thought. Peaceful, charming, bucolic even." She hated that her father had often taken her hunting when she was growing up. He had hoped she would take to it, like him. That is what alerted her. On the way, the birds had been singing. Now there was silence.

"A crime has been committed here. Both Impastato were murdered. This is concrete. I'm a journalist and I sift through their rubbish."

She could feel the danger. It was palpable, sliding down her spine. An instinctive, ancestral feeling of becoming prey. She lay down slowly in the sparse dry grass.

"If they fire on me, it's not much protection, she thought."

There was a loud bang at that moment. A split second later, a twig fell, then a shower of green olives landed around her. "Buckshot, a killer but not precise."

She slipped behind a huge olive tree which hid the hilltop. There were a lot of trees behind. "The sniper must be on the gentle slope; he can see better to shoot me."

A second shot skimmed past her ankle. She curled up behind the big trunk. "OK, it's coming from this side, that's a good thing. If they are two, I've had it. I can't stay here. One or two, either way, my only chance is to run like the hare, zigzagging as fast as I can." She was oddly calm and clear-thinking, and strangely, was aware of it. She was still full of the thriller Marathon man she had seen in the cinema. Dustin Hoffman had managed to distance himself from the killers by running. Her only chance. "Me too, it's my trump card. With my fitness, I will give him a run for his money. Go on! Go for it!"

Leaving behind her camera, she leaped up and started to run towards the town, zigzagging between the olive trees, jumping over tree stumps and stones. She heard shots but didn't take any notice. She heard the branches showered with bullets but didn't stop, continuing her fast zigzag run. The shooting had stopped. The valley was widening, she was leaving the woods. There were fields ahead, as far as the eye could see, separated by a footpath. If she took it, she could run faster but would be totally exposed. She glanced over her shoulder. Two men, young, slim. "Slim, she thought, if they were short and fat, it would be easier. With a bit of luck, they'll give up." She ran onto the path as fast as she could. She had no problems breathing. "Oh no, this bloody town is so much further than I thought. I can't see anything. No bell tower, only fields. And no-one about." Behind her, the first man had reached the path. He had a shotgun in his hand. She second one was further behind. He hadn't yet left the olive grove. "He can't run and shoot at the same time. If he decides to shoot, he'll have to stop and I'll shake him off. If he continues to run, I'll increase the distance." But he continued to run and the distance didn't increase. He even looked closer. "Two hundred meters, she guessed, glancing behind her." She gave a further push. She had warmed up now and felt good. "If he can keep this up, I have Sicily's sprinting champion on my hands!" A spire appeared on the horizon, the first church in the town. "If I reach it, I'll be no safer than here. I need a plan. The church? They'll even gun me down inside, they have no respect. They will wait for me outside. And I will be trapped. My car, where is my car? Next to the main café, on the main square. My keys? There, in my pocket."

The first houses were already within striking distance. But to her right, a man in the distance was running at a right angle towards her, to bar her way. "How do they keep in touch? With a radio, of course! The one behind I can't see any longer, raised the alarm." She veered to the left, through the fields. She had slowed down. The man on her right was also in a field; the one behind was slightly further back. Three hundred or 400 meters away, maybe. She jumped from furrow to furrow. The earth was hard and dry under her feet. "Thank God I didn't put on my town shoes today," she laughed, surprised at being able to joke about it.

When she passed the first house to enter a paved road, the two men were a long way away; the second one, who had come from the right, was the nearest. Ahead in the distance, she could see the sea. She would never be able to unlock the car, to open the door, sit down and start the car. He would have ample time to adjust his weapon and shoot at her. She was running still. She was out of breath now and couldn't find a way out.

She glanced at her watch: 11.30. The local godfather always took his aperitif whilst playing cards in the main café, next to the big church. Where her car was parked. She suddenly remembered the old *mafioso* tradition of protection. She was slowing down, but it was her last chance: to fall into the wolf's mouth to avoid its fangs; she rushed into the café, sliding past the clumsy bodyguards, who hadn't seen her. The tavern was buzzing with people; they were chatting and laughing. She went straight to the main table opposite the bar and threw herself at the feet of the godfather. Using an ancestral tradition, she said, very loudly so everyone would hear her,

— I beg for your protection, Don Valentino.

Her pursuers were at the door. Valentino Cadali looked at them nastily and made a sign which meant "Buzz off, you fools!"; then, with everyone watching in the suddenly quiet café, he had to offer the protection she had requested. According to the old ritual, he vaguely remembered. It must involve offering his hand or his ring for kissing. He stretched out his paw towards Alessa with such a look of hatred that she didn't hang around afterwards. She paid her bill, picked up her things, left the keys of the car with the hotel for Hertz to collect later, took a taxi and the first flight to Rome before the Don understood what was happening. In fact, she wasn't at risk with him as once awarded his protection, he could hardly come back on his word without disapproval.

During the night, two young Cadali *mafiosi* were taking a keen look at the Fiat. They were youngsters who had just been sworn in. There was profit to be made from selling stolen hire cars. They were always clean and agencies never filed a complaint. They paid the "pizzo", the royalty fee. In Messina, they knew a dealer who would give them a good price. They had yet to prove themselves to climb the ladder of the family hierarchy. At the very moment when, having forced the lock with no trouble, they put both wires end to end, there was a blast. It spread mechanical and human remains 50 meters away, shattering windows and shop displays.

Having heard the explosion from his home where he was enjoying a week-earned rest after giving his protection the old way, the godfather blew up himself. He called a sottocapo.

— You bloody fool, you didn't get the explosive removed!

— Well, I had planned it for dawn.

— I hope for your sake you will see beyond the dawn.

He replaced the Bakelite headset with great care.

Palermo

Cadali told what had happened at the meeting in the « Cupola ». It was the meeting of the island's *mafiosi* bosses where big decisions were taken, which territories were going to whom, as well as smaller ones. Should they make this future suicide victim disappear in acid or just let him hang? One of the capi generously offered to be in charge of the journalist's disappearance. Because Cadali could no longer do it. With thanks, said the delighted *Protector*. It would be done. The Capo Dei Capi asked:

— What was the bitch called again?

— Alessa Lombardi.

— I shall be delighted to read in the press that she was mown down in the street. I hope she is well known. Let it be a lesson to other shit stirrers of her kind.

— But we are not shit, my dear, the boss of Catania objected ; he was educated.

— Yes, in a manner of speaking Don Cicio. What would you call her?

— Spoilsport.

— OK, spoilsport. In any case, her future looks grim, whatever we call her.

They laughed heartily and went on to more serious matters after this trifle.

A few days later, the Sicilian *Capo di Capi* called his American accomplice to arrange a delivery. He told him about the clever little journalist who had found a way to get him to protect her, even though he had already appointed hitmen to keep an eye on her. She really pulled a fast one on the boss and the rumors spread around the island.

— What is the name of this young lady?

— Alessa Lombardi.

— What!

— What's the matter?

— Tell me her name again?

— Alessa Lombardi.

— Can you contact your colleague, the one who sent the cleaners, quickly?

— Yes, of course. But what's the problem?

— Alessa Lombardi is the niece of the new President of the United States, Jimmy Carter.

— Well, there! Are you sure? You're not teasing me?

— She's the daughter of his wife's sister; they are very fond of each other, according to the papers. You need to move quickly if you don't want the 6th fleet and the Action Service of the CIA on your back.

— Thanks, I'll call you back.

Rome

Alessa Lombardi had returned home in Rome. She felt relatively safe as her line was on the red list, along with the address of her flat. In Rome with its two million inhabitants and far from Sicily, she felt she wasn't in too much danger. She had again looked up ancient *mafioso* practices. Once given, a boss's protection couldn't be withdrawn. It was a code of honor. What was it worth today? The best traditions were getting lost, and not only at Cosa Nostra. That made her smile and she went for a shower. It was starting to get hot in Rome. Had she known what was happening outside, she would have felt less serene. A commando of six men surrounded the building. This time, there was no possibility of escape. But she didn't know this and was singing under the cool water. Then she got dressed to go out. She had an appointment with a new boyfriend. While she was dressing up with a summer dress and light shoes, the killers were lying in wait. The boss was the passenger in one of three cars, each with two men. He was parked 50 meters from the main entrance of the building. The two gangsters had their machine-guns handy. Not in full sight, so as not to be noticed by passers-by. When she came out, they would charge and pulverize her. In the street. Those were the orders. A warning shot for all the journalists not wise enough to report on anything other than trifles. Alessa closed the apartment door behind her. Yes, she had her keys and her handbag. She could go. Looking forward to this interlude with her lover after the horrors she had experienced in Sicily. She called the lift. In one of the cars, the boss's radio vibrated.

— Yes, said the *capodecina*.

— Abort, said a well-known voice!

— OK.

He called the other two vehicles. One car responded, the other didn't. Alessa was in the hallway and making her way to the exit. She was parked on the right, one hundred meters away. When she got into the street, the team of *soldati,* who had been warned, was keeping still. But it was useless because there were guys watching the back of the building. The third car, which had not received the message to abort, was parked 50 meters away, opposite that of the *capodecina.*

The two men inside saw Alessa come out and turn her back on them to walk quickly towards her car. They started up quietly. She had not noticed them. The passenger was holding his machine-gun poised, the window was down. "The boss, over there, is leaving it to us. It's easier to surprise a target from behind. The boss is right," thought the driver. But the boss had set off fast and was driving towards them. At the very moment the gunman was pulling the trigger, both cars crashed into each other, causing dents and losing bullets. Alessa was already in her car and on her way. She had naturally heard a noise behind her, but she didn't want to be the witness of a tedious road incident which would have spoiled her evening.

— You can't even keep your radio on in the middle of an operation, yelled the boss.

Two months before - Rome

Aldo Moro didn't know he had only left 54 days to live. When he woke up on the morning of March 16, he felt fulfilled. He had achieved what he had wanted for years, the political alliance with his longstanding rival, the Communist Party. Later, in the House of Representatives, it would be done. It was a historic moment for a historic compromise. With a crushing majority of representatives, it would provide stability to lead the country, his pipe dream.

The leader of the Communists, Ernesto Berlinguer was no ordinary communist. He was the only one who had disapproved of the invasions by the Russians of Hungary and Czechoslovakia. The two men had got on. Rivals but not enemies.

Later, the government would not vote against rightist government. It was a start: to begin a collaboration and see where it would lead. To accustom the country to not have panic-induced fear of the Reds. But the communists were terrifying, Stalin, Mao, Pol Pot. To the Church and the Italian politicians, Berlinguer was playing a game. He turned into a lamb to get into the house. No-one believed in his good faith. Apart from Moro.

And yet, Moro had been president of the Council five times. He was unavoidable, even if it was felt that he was being taken for a ride by Berlinguer.

The car was now in the northern suburbs of Rome, escorted by five carabinieri. He thought on:

"But the screwballs on the left are excited by Mao Zedong's cleansing hysteria. He lit the fuse with his 'Cultural' Revolution where culture rhymes with mass murders. This madness spread to Cambodia."

There was a bottle neck, as so often in the capital. "To the Red brigades, I am *vermin to exterminate*,' as Mao preaches. Brrr, he shivered, thank goodness I have the carabinieri to protect me."

The columned started to move, the traffic jam cleared. They were running well. He recognized the Via Mario Fani he often drove through. A pretty avenue on the heights. Cedar trees, pines shaded small residential three or four storied blocks of flats.

"It must be good to live here, he thought. In twenty minutes, we will arrive at the Montecitorio Palace."

But suddenly, in the give way sign of the crossroad with the via Stresa, a car stopped dead in front of them,

blocking them to a standstill. At the same time, gun
crackled. To his right, two motor-carabinieri fell befor
they had time to get out their weapons. He got the
impression that there was also shooting behind him. He
stretched out on his seat. He could no longer see anything.
The shootings stopped. The front door opened violently,
he straightened up a little and saw his driver collapse from
a shotgun bullet to his temple. The back door had opened
behind him. He felt pulled by his ankles like a bag of linen.
His gaze and his awareness clouded over suddenly. It was
March 16.

May 10, 1978 - Rome

On May 10, 1987, two months after Aldo Moro's
murder, Alessa Lombardi went to the *Fendinebbia* where a
few journalists and admin staff were having discussions.
The body of Moro had been found, the day before in the
boot of a car which had been symbolically parked
between the HQ of the CD and the ICP, to point to the
real perpetrators of the crime.

— It's got the sophist trademark of the Brigade
members! We didn't kill anyone. You are the oppressors,
you killed your accomplice Moro by refusing to free our

comrades you kidnapped and
n camps.

'le of their nine convoluted press
......al propaganda gruel. All of life's
complex situations must, willingly or not, fit into their
thought patterns.

— All the same, it's awful for his family. Two months
of suffering! Have you read his letters? They are poignant.
He's asking his CD colleagues to negotiate his release in
exchange for the release of Brigade members. All along
his colleagues pretended not to have heard anything. They
could have saved him.

— State reasons. To negotiate with the Red Brigades
is to recognize them politically. To release ideological
terrorists would risk the stability of society, already
weakened. Can the rule of law give in to blackmail without
destroying itself slowly?

— You make me laugh with your high political
principles! Neither Bodrotti nor the Home Secretary nor
Paul VI lifted a finger to negotiate and save Moro! He was
the leader of the left wing of the CD, the creator of the
historic compromise with the ICP, an ideology Bodrotti
and the Pope were far from sharing. Moro's death didn't
bother them much.

— The CIA would have been involved, having
infiltrated and manipulated the Red Brigades.

— The CIA is no choirboy. But from there to see
their hand everywhere. The far left is spreading these

rumors. Only the CIA can commit such a base action! Our brave and pure Brigade members could never do such a thing! When we all know what they are capable of. Their brothers are doing it in Cambodia: two million dead in three years! The Maoist far left is worse, while appearing as innocent as a pastor boy. Have you spoken to the wives and kids of the five men murdered on March 16!?

— It's still odd that the security services didn't find out where Moro was being held.

— Yes, it's making a lot of people wonder what went on. A good explanation is often the simplest. But one gets treated like an idiot who understands nothing. The hideaway? An ordinary flat in Rome. A needle in a haystack. If the Brigade members apply the security criteria of a network in a hostile country, it works. Militarily speaking, the attack on March 16 was faultless. The escape, too. They disappeared within Rome on that day. That's what the police assumed from the beginning. If the terrorists don't make a mistake, if there are no snitches, if the police don't have informers in the area, it's very difficult to spot. The Red Brigades are trained to stay in hiding. They train in the USSR, in China, in Bulgaria, who knows? The cartridges were from Czechoslovakia.

— It has been said that the hideaway was found and they deliberately didn't intervene. To allow Moro to be killed.

— Say what you like, it's your choice. But again, I think it's absurd. Can you imagine the kudos of the government had they managed to free Moro and arrest the Red Brigades? This hypothesis is as unlikely as that of the CIA. The culprits can only be the authorities, the Church or the CIA. Whereas in fact, the Red Brigades have a utopian ideology, that of the Khmer Rouges. We must avoid giving them any leverage. The government had to decide. Abandon Moro to a certain death, to nip it in the bud so as not to let it develop as it has elsewhere. Bodrotti and Dossica, not my favorite people, had no choice. Take Chamberlain and Churchill before the war. Chamberlain, looking for peace and humanity, and to avoid war, allowed Hitler to grow. We know what happened then. Leaders are sometimes made to accept one death to prevent others.

— Your cold cynicism is pretty disgusting. Can you imagine what Moro went through during the two months? The attitude of the government and of Berlinguer was cruel.

— Yes, hugely cruel. To avoid even more cruelty. Horrid. It was about choosing between a certain, immediate murder and hundreds of thousands of uncertain deaths. We'll never know.

— In other words, a moral dilemma? It reminds me of Lorenzaccio by Musset or Dirty Hands by Sartre.

— We are talking a lot about Moro, but we are not mentioning Peppino Impastato's murder only yesterday.

— Who?

— A young and courageous Sicilian idealist. He had decided to stand up to the Mafia in his town, Cinisi near Palermo. He had founded a radio station where he mocked the local godfather and *mafiosi*. He was standing for the local elections due in a week. Against the CD supported by Bodrotti, and by Cosa Nostra. He died yesterday, in the middle of the election campaign. His blown-up body was found on the railway line. The exiting municipality states that Peppino Impastato was trying to blow up the line and got it wrong; no-one believed that, of course. He was from a *mafiosi* family, from Father to Son. As a young man, he saw his uncle's remains spread about a dozen fruit trees; he was traumatized. If that's what the mafia were like, he wanted nothing to do with it. Until last year, he was still protected by his father, a *mafioso* who begged the local boss to spare his son. To get peace, the godfather had the Impastato father taken out last year. Then he could blow up his son without being bothered by his father's whining. Sicily is like that: it's worthy of our Roman dramas, don't you think? I'm off there tomorrow, to write a paper. I hope to come back alive. Otherwise, come to my funeral, all of you, bearing anti-octopus's slogans.

THE CHIMERA

1957 – 1974

1957 – Palermo

Twenty-one years earlier, in Palermo.

It was in the suite of New York boss Gambino, at Palm Palace.

— We're going to triple our heroin sales! Let him in!

Sindona stepped forward and kissed his hand.

— Good morning, Don Carlo, thanks for receiving me.

The other exclaimed in Sicilian dialect:

— You're clearly working wonders to turn our funds into outstanding capital.

— Thank you, Don Carlo, I'm flattered answered Sindona, also in Sicilian.

His was from Messina, they understood each other, they moved in the same circles.

Lucky Luciano, dressed in a light suit was having a drink just a bit further away. The latest capo of Capi, maybe still the current one, no-one knew, looked like a retired dentist. Two bodyguards in dark suits stood nearby.

Carlo Gambino was a small man, with dark black hair combed backwards and dark eyes. Born in Palermo, he had emigrated to the United States during the fascist era and had climbed to the top of the crime fraternity. Initially as killer for godfathers, later as killer of godfathers. A classic CV, not unlike the one of the dentist nearby, organizer of this Italo-American gangster's high gathering.

Michele Sindona, the mob manager, was slim and elegant; he had done well at school. Whereas Gambino could hardly read or write. But he knew how to kill and how to have others killed. Which he had just inflicted on his boss while he was taking a shave in the Sheraton. And then, two weeks later, to his partner. As these things got known, he was shown more respect than his educational pathway would have warranted.

— We are going to take our business to the next level, said Gambino. We are going to shore up our financial sector. I want to trust you with this very important task for our family. Do you agree? And if so, how do you think we should set it up?

This was an offer that no-one could turn down. And Sindona was very keen to say yes.

He went on:

— The more important the sums of money, the more complex and expensive the recycling. When we wash $100,000, we only get $80,000. The ratio falls to 70% for a million dollars. For a hundred million dollars, it won't exceed 60%.

Luciano was listening. Unlike Gambino, he knew all about these ratios. He looked at Gambino and nodded.

— Good, you're hired, said Gambino to Sindona. You'll give back 60 cents, as white as snow, for every dollar we entrust you with. The other 40% are your fees and salary. They have nothing to do with me. You do as you wish. Your only commitment will be to change 100 underground to 60 on the surface. You OK with that?

— Yes, Don, it's simple and generous. One question: do you want a delay between the entrance at 100 and the refund at 60?

Gambino looked at Luciano who gave him an evasive glance.

— How long would you give it, Gambino asked Sindona?

— Between six and twenty-four months depending on the complexity of the work. This time delay ensures an inscrutable and secure laundering.

Gambino glanced again at Luciano who had lit a cigarette and didn't seem to be with them anymore. As he listened to everything, it meant approval.

OK. You're the family's financial manager now. See Don Rosario about the details. Andrea, you can tell him to come in. Silvio, bring the champagne!

Rosario entered, as they were preparing the flutes.

— Smiling, Gambino said: it's done. Thank you for introducing Michele. He'll do an excellent job. We agreed on a 60% lump sum. OK with you?

Rosario Di Maggio was head of the Passo di Rigano family and one of the most influential godfathers in Palermo, but Gambino was his superior. So, it was fine with him. If he had said 40%, it would still have been fine for him.

1960 – Milano

Milan's archbishop, Giovanni Montini was feeling low. He'd been moping for six years in his position, albeit the most prestigious in Italy. That swine Pie XII had gotten rid of him, by making him Bishop there. But Montini wanted to become pope, not Bishop of Milan! He had served Pie XII in Rome for more than ten years. He had seen at close hand what power meant. He wanted it. And he found it difficult to conceal it. When Pie XII had died two years previously, he still hadn't been appointed cardinal. And this stood on his way to Saint

Peter's throne. Angelo Roncalli had stolen his place, under the name of John XXIII; a good man who had promoted him right away.

Nevertheless, the finally appointed Cardinal Montini still champed at the bit. Building churches and blessing nurseries didn't have the same cachet as being God's representative on earth. He was already 63 years old. His last chance would come when Pope John, already 80, died. He had to be ready. Maintain his networks.

Thank goodness, he had his personal secretary, Father Pasquale Macchi, to lift his spirits when he felt low. At 37, he was like a son to him. Even more than that. He picked up his phone.

— Hello, Mr. Sindona, could we meet?

— Of course, your Eminence, as soon as you like.

Michele Sindona met Cardinal Montini at the archbishopric. Their faces were alike. Thin with prominent and fine noses, and intense sunken eyes. Montini wanted to open a nursing home for deprived people. He didn't have the funds and the banks wouldn't lend.

— How much money do you need for that charity, Eminence, asked the Cosa Nostra financier?

— Two and a half million dollars, said the prelate.

— I'll see what I can do. You'll get an answer in a few days.

His mind was made up. "Montini could become pope. I'll dip into my slush funds. If he becomes pope, this gamble will pay off. If not, it can still be useful to be the friend of Milan's Cardinal-archbishop."

Ten days later, the cash was credited to the archbishop's account. It was a loan from a foreign bank, without interest, of unlimited duration and with no depreciation.

— Alleluia, cried out Montini, God is showing his choice for his next vicar!

1969 – the Vatican

Nine years later, the two men had become friends and had fulfilled their dreams. But their features had aged. Montini had been elected pope in 1963, becoming Paul VI.

Paul Marcinkus, his bodyguard, was becoming too inquisitive of his private life; he appointed him bishop and head of the Vatican Bank, to get rid of him. But Marcinkus, a bruiser from the Chicago slums knew nothing about banking. All he could do was play golf, smoke cigars, swing a baseball bat and get into fights.

The old pope Pie XII had bought loads of shares in Italian companies. He wanted to control Italy. But this papal wealth was palpable. It created discontent in the country. Paul VI decided to get rid of them. Not by giving them to the poor, but by sending them abroad. If the Church was to continue its donations to charitable organizations forever, world without end, it could only do so by remaining prosperous. Not by becoming poor!

— Mr. Sindona, could I see you with Bishops Marcinkus?

The four men, including Father Machi gathered. The pope disclosed his intention to reduce the clergy's wealth in Italy.

— Let's start with shares, as Italy wants to tax our dividends. On Milan's stock exchange, what is the value of our 20% in Societa Generale Immobiliare, our 60% in Condotte d'Acqua, distribuing water in Rome as well as our minority control in Ceramica Possi?

Sindona and Macchi made a rough calculation: 20 million dollars.

— Would you be interested in the lot, the pope asked Sindona?

— Yes, Holy Father, and I'll offer you 25 million.

It was another multiplication of the loaves. Paul VI slipped a word to his secretary to offer a prayer of thanksgiving at vespers. Cosa Nostra would pay the 25 million. It was going to be complex to split the capital flow in transit, needing brass-plate companies and banks from various countries. Sindona had acquired quite a few. The Mafia would inject 25 dirty millions and recuperate 15, white as heroin. The 10 million dollars difference would be shared between Sindona, Calvi and Marcinkus. Discounts would go to facilitators like the poisonous Elio Cighi, the P2 lodge Venerable, as well as American *mafiosi*. Organized crime was buying the Vatican's Italian goods in this smokescreen, while laundering the funds. The mob wouldn't be getting the same shares. They would be given other assets than the three initial lots of shares. These would be split up, repackaged in the wastewater treatment plant, and resold to international investors, suckers who would pay high prices for them. Same as Texon, close to Credit Suisse, who would then reinject the dirty money into Italy for its … Italian clients.

Many identical operations took place later on. The emptying of the Italian Church portfolio and the laundering took place, hand in hand. The Holy Father was recycling heroin money.

March 1974 - New York

Five years later, Michele Sindona was sitting opposite his Creator. Don Carlo Gambino, the Capo dei tutti Capi, had changed since 1957 when the two of them had met for the first time in Palermo. He was now seventy years old and, with a heart condition, was showing his age.

— Well, Michele, what do you have to tell me?

Sindona decided to come clean. It was no use to start messing about.

— Don Carlo, I gambled and I lost. My financial empire is falling apart. It's like a sand castle caught by the rising tide. I have no excuse. Apart from underestimating the devastating power of the oil crisis. Even the mightiest were affected. My system wasn't strong enough. It was built to deal with normal forecasting. Not fit for the financial and economic hurricane we are experiencing. I am taking responsibility for this.

— I appreciate your honesty, said the boss.

Gambino turned towards his Consigliere.

— How much money do we have in Michele's system?

— Sixty million dollars after laundering.

— Can you give it back, Gambino asked Sindona?

The only possible answer was yes. No would mean death.

— Yes, said Sindona. I have some advice and a request, Don Carlo.

— I'm listening.

— My system is rotten. I have to abandon ship. Would it be possible not to submit any more funds as from now on? I can offer no guarantee for the future. It's OK for the past but not for the future.

— Is this possible, Consigliere?

— We can close the debit system within three to four days.

— Can we cope elsewhere?

— Yes, we've got spare wheels.

Gambino got back to Sindona.

— Good. Michele, when are you going to give those 60 million back to the family?

— By this week. All I need is an account number.

— All right. Consigliere, please give it to Michele.

He got up, hugged Sindona:

— We've done a good job together, I'm pleased. Everything comes to an end on this earth. Take care and try to cut your losses.

He sent him away after giving him his ring to kiss.

After Sindona left, Gambino told the Consigliere:

— Sindona remains in the family, but he's out as our financier. Who would you suggest for this post?

— Roberto Calvi from Ambrosiano Bank.

— OK. Get on with it.

Everybody lost in Sindona's crash, apart from the mafia. The biggest loser was the American taxpayer. Sindona, with 20% of shares, controlled the Franklin National Bank, the 20th ranked American Bank. The US Treasury came to the rescue when it was almost bankrupt, to avoid chain reactions and the systemwide shock its downfall would have created. It injected two billion dollars.

September 1974 – Rome

On September 3rd, Elio Cighi, the Venerable of P2 Lodge, received a call.

— Sindona will be arrested the day after tomorrow, I thought you might be interested.

— Thank you, my dear friend, I won't forget that one!

Then Michele Sindona received a call.

— Michele, you'll be arrested the day after tomorrow.

— Thank you, Elio. I won't forget that one!

On September 4th, Michele Sindona, who was now also a Swiss citizen, took off for Geneva. Then for the US to his suite at the hotel Pierre off Central Park.

December 1974 - Castel Gondolfo

Pope Paul VI was sunbathing under a big white wide-brimmed hat. There was hardly a sound, just a few birds singing and a helicopter in the distance. The last year hadn't been good. Oil prices had tripled. The Dow Jones had dropped by more than half. Sindona was bankrupt and on the run. France was legalizing abortion.

An empty coffee cup and yesterday's newspaper opened on page 13 stood on the coffee table next to the deckchair.

Corriere della Sera – In Switzerland, the body of a manager for "Banco di Roma for Switzerland" was found on the Lugano—Chiasso railway line. It could be a suicide as a letter to his wife was found in his pocket. This tragedy could be linked to the bank's enormous losses; half of the bank is owned by IOR and the other half by Banco di Roma.

"I'm only the temporary trustee of Saint Peter's crown, Paul VI thought, the Church will outlast me, it's already gone through so much. Today's troubles can hardly touch it. Everything will be forgotten in a few years' time. But how will I stay in people's hearts? I'm the best traveled Pope. I was proud of it. But is this enough to be a great pope?"

He went indoors where Father Macchi was waiting for him. He asked him for his advice on Sindona's fall.

— Well, he had too much leverage, answered Macchi.

Paul VI raised a questioning brow.

— Too many debts, not solid enough assets. When the price of wild investments falls and the debts don't move, it's bankruptcy.

— Can't one just wait for the markets to recover?

— No. A snowball effect unleashes. The creditors also want their money back because they need to fill the gaps, too. And even if they have no gap to fill, they demand to be paid because they fear they won't be. Justifiably. See for yourself, Sindona Group blew up in mid-flight.

— Thank you Macchi. Blindingly clear. On a similar subject, the funds used by Sindona and still used by Marcinkus and Calvi could not be that clean. What are your thoughts?

— Well, Holy Father, what is clean in finance? It is not a squeaky-clean activity in itself. Try to limit the damage, yes. But from there to throw out the baby with the bathwater.

— I'm reassured. Could you help me with remedial measures? Like verifying the . . . beverage . . . what do you call them?

— Leverages, Holy Father. Sindona's crash is a warning shot. The lure of excessive profit leads to leverage abuse. Rules have to be set for the congregations who manage the Church's money. And competent controllers chosen. The management tools have become too sophisticated for the external auditors. They don't understand what they've come to inspect. Or when they do, it's too late.

— Should we appoint qualified controllers?

— Yes, Your Holiness.

But his Holiness was already elsewhere. Macchi felt it and kept quiet.

Pope Paul was thinking: "these money matters are secondary compared to other stakes. Just let Marcinkus, Calvi and their ilk get on with it. Each to his own sector. Mine are spirituality and politics, deeply intertwined. In 1939, Pie XII didn't fight the antichrist. In those days it was embodied in Nazism and Fascism. Today, I must be careful not to make the same mistake again. The devil is with the soviets, the gulag, the communists' attempt to control the world. I must fight the devil, the rest hardly matters. I'm not going to talk about this to Macchi or anyone else, but I finally understood that Sindona, Calvi, Marcinkus and company were in bed with the Octopus. Though one can never be sure in that area. Only with the tip of its tentacles? I even wonder if Bodrotti himself isn't involved."

He drove his suspicion out. "Those rumors are only KGB fake news. To unsettle us."

Father Macchi had a rather sharper understanding of the papal thought:

"He knows, but doesn't want to deal with it. He understands the financial dealings and is not looking. He's more political than ethical. He's carrying on with what he did under Pie XII; he was a strong political element in the Curia at that time. Like Pie XII, he's a very Italian pope, de facto chief of Christian Democracy. Deep down, he's keeping the balance between the red menace and the mafia peril. So, he compromises with the latter to fight the first. The mafia is Italian, which means patriots to him; practicing Catholics who can get absolution after confession; anticommunists, so anti-Russian; maybe even underhandedly supported by the CIA; close to the right wing of Christian Democracy, the good one, Bodrotti's Christian Democracy; and willing to become prosperous. A lot of common ground between Cosa Nostra and the Church. The pope must be saying to himself: The mafia is certainly rough, but you can't make an omelet without breaking eggs.

THE SNAKE

1969 – 1977

1976 - the Vatican

Young banker Vittorio Petri, who had been working for two years at the IOR, the Institute for the Works of Religion, usually called the Vatican Bank, had recovered from a serious road traffic accident. His uncle, Albino Luciani, the Cardinal-bishop of Venice, had recommended him to the director Bishop Paul Marcinkus. Vittorio Petri knew finance, which he had dealt with in Switzerland, inside out. In particular, deals which were outside the bounds of legality. He climbed fast up the echelons and became one of the boss's assistants.

November 1976 - Maryland (USA)

Nancy Jones, professor of cryptography at Bern University, was seen by the director of encryption and the director of the NSA.

— Nancy, I am happy to see you back with us. Good flight?

— Perfect, thank you. And what about you both, your families, are you all well?

— Yes, thank you, both men replied. Your friend Vittorio has recovered, you said. Excellent news. Unfortunately, we don't have much time. Shall we start?

— Of course.

— President-elect, Jimmy Carter, gave me a mission that we need to deal with straightaway, continued the director of the NSA. The exiting president Gerald Ford made his agreement. The President-Elect has received briefings on our allies, our antagonists and everything else. One thing caught his eye. It's the extent of connivance that might remain between the CIA and Cosa Nostra. We made the mistake, in 1943, to collaborate with the mafia to invade Sicily. As if we could not have managed on our own! Later, the fear of the reds persisted, increased because zones had been shared out at Yalta. Italy and Greece were in the zone under the West's influence. Unlike Czechoslovakia, Hungary, Poland, etc. which were given over to the Soviet bloc. So, Stalin didn't support

Greek, Portuguese or Italian communists. And we did nothing for democrats from the Eastern bloc. Everyone was his master at home. That is what Yalta was. But it was a secret.

The President-Elect wants to know whether our connivance, or as the case may be, our complicity, persists even today. Of course, total silence with the CIA. Because they are the ones Carter suspects.

— Thank you, Paul. What about me, though, asked Nancy?

The encryption boss explained:

— We would like you to become the director of Rome. Its membership will increase. It will tune into the Italian state and the Vatican; its main representatives, politics, army, police force, financial affairs, episcopate and the *mafiosi* godfathers will be identified. It's 100% classified. Our allies need not be in the know, any more than the CIA; and neither does your boyfriend.

— Depending on what we find, Carter will decide, explained the director. For now, he just wants to know. He doesn't want to be thrown any old stuff as with Kennedy, with the attack on Cuba at the Bay of Pigs.

— Fine, I agree, said Nancy. When? Why me? What's my cover?

— It is now November 18. 1st December at the latest, would that suit you?

— Yes.

— You, because it's you. And because you produced the latest "backdoors" on the coders of crypto AG. The Swiss firm has sold its machines to the Italians, in the public and in the private sectors. You will make a better sense of the machines and of the info. Especially since your colleagues mustn't know anything about the "hidden doors". So, you will be very much alone.

— I'm used to this, it doesn't bother me.

— For your cover, you have just been appointed Professor of Cryptography at the University of Rome, a friendly exchange with Bern. You will have two hours' lecture per week and a few exams. No follow-on thesis. As for the mentorship, you will be well supported.

— May I live with my fellow?

— Yes, you can even sleep together if you like, the director replied, not without humor.

— You have not forgotten the bodyguard jokes of your youth, Paul, it's very pleasing to see you still have your way with words!

— Vittorio, darling, we are going to be able to live together again if you like. I have a job in Rome, hooray!

— Wow, Fabulous, Nancy! The flat seems empty without you. When are you coming?

— Very soon. Bern is letting me go. I am appointed in Rome. A similar post.

— Congratulations! Still a professor of Crypto?

— Yes.

— Ordinary or extraordinary?

— Ordinary. Its stable and allows me to continue with my research. This sector changes so quickly! If you don't pull out all the stops, you regress and become a "has been" in a year.

— Wonderful darling. When can we see each other?

— If I move next week, will that do?

— Perfetto. Big hug.

— Me too. And you? I forgot with my little self. How are you? And work?

— Bene, I'll tell you all about it. Physically, I have recovered well. I take strenuous walks, I'm feeling good, I don't have any pain. Almost an odd sensation!

— See you next week, I'll come by car. I'll let you know which day, so we can book a romantic table. In the Trastevere?

— OK.

Winter 1977 - Milan

Journalist Alessa Lombardi was reading press cuttings. She felt so downcast that she was relieved to hear the library closing.

The story she was investigating was deadly. How could this have happened? To what end? Who?

The next day she took a walk. In the midst of these articles, trials, invectives from all sides, multiple bombings since 1969, the truth could only come out of known facts. They were so fragmented. She would do better to think of the strategy used by the murderers and link it to similar past events.

The wave of blast murders had started on 12 December 1969. The explosion at the Banca Nazionale dell'Agricoltura, on the Piazza Fontana in Milan had killed 17 and wounded 88 people. On that day, four identical attacks had taken place in Milan and in Rome. They were clearly linked. The economic and political capitals.

Alessa recalled the fire at the Reichstag in 1933, ordered by Hitler and apportioned to the communists in order to establish his dictatorship. The attacks of 12 December 1969 against "capitalistic" targets were also under a *fake banner*, so that they would be attributed to the far left. This was the method of the Nazis everywhere: to exploit fear or, failing that, to create it. The security reflex of the population next called for fascist law and order.

The ingredients were there in 1969: mass arrests of left-wingers, defenestration of a suspect anarchist arrested by the police. A so-called suicide. The dead plead guilty and keep quiet.

A guilty anarchist would never commit suicide. To the contrary, he would have claimed the moral legitimacy of his armed fight against bourgeois totalitarianism.

"Eight years of terror have gone by since 69", thought Alessa. And democracy didn't collapse. People are still under the spell after the twenty-five years of mussolinian dictatorship. All these small groups at both extremes! Impossible to find guilty parties in that lot, looking for a needle, etc. On the other hand, could deduction?

The far right. Crime wore its trademark, even when disguised as left-wing attacks. Neo-fascist factions don't have the intellectual acumen to set up a global scenario of destabilization. They are good murderers, but also very stupid.

Elio Cighi, for his part, has the capacity to be a sponsor. His past and current presentation are a good fit. He never leaves anything in writing, no evidence. He will never be directly implicated, he's too careful. He incites others. He has always remained unblemished even in the center of his thick web. So thick that no-one knows whether it really exists. Like black holes in the galaxy, it seems. One would only know about them through emanations on the periphery.

And Andrea Bodrotti, the leader of the right-wing of the CD? Though perhaps not. He has the brains and the moral turpitude, but in the event of a fascist coup, the ultras would overflow on his right. And he knows it. Exit Bodrotti. Same for the royalists, the fanatics would replace them. Like King Constantine of Greece in 1967, during the colonels' takeover. And like von Papen by Hitler in 1933.

One of these days, I'll throw a cat among the pigeons: Cighi could be the sponsor of the Piazza Fontana. Try it out and see their reaction. I search his past, sign under a pseudonym and get out.

She remembered an anecdote from the previous year. She couldn't find the cutting. It was short. A prosecutor who was working on the attacks had been mown down in the street. So, he had been close to finding the truth. End of the inquiry. The article referred to his widow. If she could find the headline, she could interview her.

She found it at last. It was in July 1976 in Rome. The victim was Vittorio Occorsio, a stand-in. - ... *he was looking into the links between a Neo-fascist group and the P2 lodge. . .*

— Assassination, neo-Nazi small group, P2 lodge, Elio Cighi, bingo! she cried aloud.

— Hello, I am Alessa Lombardi. Are you Mrs. Occorsio?

— Si

— I am a freelance journalist. I mainly write articles for the bimonthly journal Fendinebbia. Do you know it?

— No.

— As its title suggests, the journal takes a broad view of current affairs and tries to provide insight. In my capacity, I am trying to make sense of the terrorist wave which is affecting us since the Piazza Fontana in 69. As your late husband did. Please accept my condolences.

— Grazie.

— Would you agree to meet me?

Beep beep beep. She had put down the receiver.

"Too painful, thought Alessa, she lost her man too recently. But it's also too dangerous. She knew in her bones what it was. Serve me right. But the reaction of Signora Occorsio shows me her husband was close to the truth."

Fabio, the chief reporter and Alessa stood in an unbelievable muddle at the headquarters of Fendinebbia. They couldn't even find a chair that was not covered in papers, newspapers, books and printers balancing on these towers of Babel. She had found the corner of a desk on which to sit while he moved about while gesticulating among the piles arising from the floor.

— Each time I come over, I wonder how you manage with your filing system, smiled Alessa.

— Don't change the subject! We were talking about your article. It's brilliant, you have amazing intuitions which are mostly right, it's well rounded, captivating, but there is no question of publishing such an incendiary piece. Do you want to set fire to Italy and sink the journal at the same time? Is that your secret plan? Tell me, he added, after spinning around a pile of magazines and staring squarely at the journalist.

— Have you finished? Are you feeling better? Can we talk sensibly?

— Yes, but you are going to give me a heart attack. Would you like some coffee?

— With pleasure. No sugar, thank you. And thank you for the compliments. This is the problem with this country. When you get close to the truth, you risk your career at best, your life at worst. I can give you an insight on the optimal cooking time of spaghetti if that's what you want. The journal will not be in danger. But you will not sell many copies.

— Stop it, stop it. You know that deep down I agree with you; we just need to find a way to stay on top of things. To survive editorially. And physically too. You can't name Elio Cighi. You have no proof. In court, he would make mincemeat of us!

— Have you seen his antecedents? A fascist fighter for Franco in Spain, a black shirt for Mussolini, a collaborator of the SS, a thief of the treasury of Yugoslavia, Grandmaster of the occult lodge Propaganda Due, and there's more. He is so secretive that we don't know much.

— But you can't accuse someone of multiple murders without evidence! What can we establish? His activities in Spain? Many Italians have fought in Spain, and that is not considered a crime. His fascist activities? Same. Except that there have been many others, still active. His past as a collaborator? You show them! Even the Communists supported him in 1945. Go find out why. His business selling mattresses? It's no crime to sell mattresses! Your story about the Yugoslav treasury? Not a shadow of proof! At a legal level, this is unfounded gossip. Just like this lodge P2. There too, they make up, they love to build stories in Italy. Twenty percent turn out to be true. Eighty percent are false. That's the point of our journal. Sort the wheat from the chaff. I'm not going to the wire with no evidence. Or, at the very least, a bundle of solid clues.

— Nice speech. You sound like the opposition. It's interesting that you talk about bundles when we are talking about fascism. Have you been infected?

Fabio hovered between irritation and pacification. He chose the latter.

— Good. What about writing two completely separate articles in the same copy?

— How?

— In the first article, you pick up what you were planning to write but you make no allegation. Nor of P2. In the second, signed with a different name, we mention the career of one Cighi. Only what is known, verifiable and public. People will make the link for themselves. No need for a picture. Legally, it's watertight.

— Clever. OK.

*

— Hi, Elio, this encoder you made me buy is brilliant! Once you get the measure of it, it can be connected to the phone, radio or telex. Very expensive but worth it. I'm calling you to practice and to thank you.

— I'm pleased you're happy with it. I have used it for years. As with cars, I would advise you to change it for the latest model. The engineer of *Crypto* often comes to carry out the updates. The after sales service is typically Swiss, that is to say, perfect. But a little bird tells me that you are not calling me just to practice.

— Your little bird is right. Have you seen the latest copy of *Fendinebbia*?

— Yes, not very flattering for me.

— And the other article on the Piazza Fontana, have you read it?

— Yes.

— Do you want us to take action?

Even with the Swiss encoding, they didn't like to call a spade a spade. It was the result of many years of criminal and illegal acts. Their communication was indirect.

— Take action?

— The reporter, it seems her health is precarious.

— These are just rumors. From what I know, she is in excellent health. She is efficient. Pity she's not with us.

— And the chief reporter?

— He, too, is in good health. I wish him a long and wonderful life. You see, what would people think if the health of the reporter, or the reporter in chief, started to fail suddenly, after such an action?

— They would think, quite wrongly, that you would have something to feel guilty about in the misfortune that would befall them.

— There you are. We keep quiet. We don't react. No indignation. No court proceedings. Let sleeping dogs lie. We don't exist.

April 1977 - Zurich

Ernst Kuhrmeier, director of the Credit Suisse (CS) of Chiasso, had set up Texon sixteen years earlier. After flourishing for years, it was now bringing ruin to the CS. The loss stood at around 2.5 billion Swiss francs. Kuhrmeier was summoned to Zurich before the directors of the bank. "Close" to the CS, Texon laundered suspicious Italian funds. Texon's investments, recycled through Italian firms, had become sour. The oil crisis had created a chain reaction of bankruptcies. Kuhrmeier talked for a long while.

— I have received explicit death threats against you, my colleagues and myself. They come from people hurt by this fiasco. If the CS does not reimburse them fully. Those who have come out of the woodwork are not being fair, it is not their style. The godfathers have squeaky clean intermediaries. They present well and are smart looking.

The threat must be taken seriously. It is not only the Swiss financial system which is at risk. It is your lives.

He paused, then started again.

— The public will remain convinced that you knew nothing. My close guard and myself are the only targets. We are not complaining about that. I have set up this business, I'll deal with it. You, the general directors and members of the Administrative Council, you will just be officially responsible. But not guilty.

You were aware of Texon's operations from the start. That was fourteen years ago. You kept your eyes closed. You let it happen. Year after year, you cashed in the huge profits Texon was transferring to the CS. You have encouraged, congratulated and rewarded us.

I am giving you a warning and know that I'm well informed. If you don't return the money, you are all condemned to death. It is not very Swiss-like to say that, particularly in high finance. But it's the law in the Mezzogiorno. It's impossible to sort out whom to reimburse and not reimburse. It's too untidy. One doesn't know who's who. The only solution is to pay ALL the clients. And soon. If one started to nitpick in order to save a few hundreds of millions here and there, it would just take one omission, even worth only 50,000 francs, for a contract to be arranged against you. For those not in the know, a contract is an order given by a chief *mafioso* to killers to take out one or several people. We have reached, you have reached an invisible, virtual barrier. Like it or not, we have entered the world of organized crime. And that world is implacable.

A leaden silence fell around the huge meeting table.

— In short? You need to monopolize your internal reserves. You need to accept the three billion bridging loan, offered by the SNB about which you are being picky. You need to accept the offer of help from our big competitors; without maneuvering or delaying any further. If you wait a day longer, and I mean one day, the withdrawals of clients, already substantial, will become a whirlwind.

And you and I, our wives and our children, will have nowhere in the world to hide. Act before tomorrow! It's a warning.

Then Kuhrmeier went quiet. Members started to whisper in small groups. Then the president thanked Kuhrmeier for his candid words and asked him to withdraw. The police escort which had brought him in, met him at the door.

The next day, the CS gave in. It committed all its reserve stock. It accepted every bit of help from the SNB and its competitors. It dealt with everything, the entire short-changed client base. All would be reimbursed, in full and quickly. The shares of the CS, which had been shot from the top to zero, bounced back.

After this, Swiss banks passed an agreement with the central bank, the SNB, that they had to know their clients.

An elementary principle pompously called: "Know your customer". They also had to abstain from laundering criminal money. Such an elementary principle that one didn't know what to call it formally.

May 1977 - Venice

Cardinal Albino Luciani, archbishop of Venice, hugged his nephew Vittorio Petri.

— What a pleasure to welcome you, what news are you bringing from Rome? You look as fit as a fiddle. You're no longer in pain?

— No, Uncle, said Vittorio, happy to see his smiling, simple and warm relative despite his elevated position. I am cured. Thanks to your support, to your affection.

— You would have recovered without me, don't be silly! Shall we go to the Lido, we can hire bikes? We could stop at a café.

— With pleasure. In Rome it's not easy to get out into the countryside.

Albino Luciani took off his cassock, donned shorts and a shirt. They set off to catch a vaporetto.

— What about your friend Nancy, is she getting used to life in Rome?

— Yes, and she likes the work. We are happy to be together again.

— Can you see how the light plays on the waves? Ah, here we are. You coming?

They pedaled towards Chioggia. At the end of the Lido, they stepped into a vaporetto. Swordfish was always skillfully prepared at the Albergo di Chioggia.

— You're still happy with your work? asked Albino to Vittorio.

— Yes, and I am grateful that you introduced me to the IOR. I am respected and well paid; it's not about me. But the higher I go, the more I am surprised at what I see. Rome is the capital of Catholicism, but there are some pretty "unorthodox", shady things going on there.

— Are you allowed to tell me about this?

— I am held to confidentiality. But some transactions do surprise me. You know what I did in Switzerland and how much it cost me. I'm not going to do it again, don't worry.

— Don't tell me anything. But I got you into this, perhaps I shouldn't have. Beware of Bishop Marcinkus and of Roberto Calvi, from the Ambrosiano bank. Don't put your nose in things that could harm you. There are plenty of jobs in your field.

— Thank you.

— Long before you arrived in Italy, Michele Sindona had built a global financial empire. He worked closely with Marcinkus and Calvi. Three years ago, his empire collapsed in a fraudulent way. He escaped to the United States. The other two are still there and still powerful. Be careful now you have been promoted. Before, as a junior, you were invisible. Now, you need to take care.

On the way back, Vittorio Petri pondered that his uncle was extraordinarily simple and authentic. The more he was immersed in the Vatican's pretentious pomp, the more he admired him.

"That man in front, pedaling in shorts and shirt, with just a distinctive Roman collar, that man is the archbishop and cardinal of Venice. He looks as though he doesn't care. He doesn't only look like it, he really doesn't care. What a man!"

Vittorio was thinking about all the things he couldn't say. The suitcases full of cash brought to the counters. Big transfers into and out of the Banco Ambrosiano. The enormous losses the IOR had nearly sustained in the Texon/CS affair.

THE GOAT

August 6—September 4, 1978

August 1978 – Rome

On August 6, Alessa Lombardi scribbled in her notebook:

« Death of Paul VI. He would be remembered as someone ill at ease, tormented and wavering. This guy had wanted so badly to become pope! But even as a bishop, he had reached his level of incompetence. On birth control, Wojtyla held the pen. And on money laundering, Sindona & Co. »

Thursday August 24, 1978 – the Vatican

The Roman month of August was scorching even in the Vatican's shady gardens. The following day, the

111 cardinal electors would be locked up in the Sistine Chapel, with windows sealed and without air conditioning until a pope emerged. These conditions would ensure a short conclave. The Venetian cardinal-archbishop Albino Luciani had arrived in his old Lancia which had broken down on his arrival in Rome.

— Could you have it repaired as quickly as possible, Vittorio? I would like to get back to Venice as soon as we have a new pope.

— Don't worry Uncle, I will see to it. Your old banger hasn't given up yet. Is your accommodation comfortable?

— Yes. But the cells of the Sistine Chapel are quite Spartan. To ensure a quick vote if the heat wave doesn't do it.

— What does the conclave look like?

— There is never an obvious candidate. It would be inconvenient. They would give themselves away at the outset. There are no negotiations. It all comes from the Holy Spirit when the time comes. You pray, you give masses, you discuss. But you don't negotiate. You talk. You come up with the ideal pontiff, and as if by a miracle, he matches exactly an existing prelate. You don't say "Vote for John", you draw an accurate depiction of him and you understand.

— Are there parties, trends, cliques as the press seem to say?

— A bit of all this. Two very distinctive groups always emerge at each election. The conservative clan, mainly traditionalist, even retrograde. And the liberal party, which would appreciate a more collegiate management, a Church more open to modern society, with less wealth. Between these two poles, neither of them having a majority of two thirds, lies the Marsh. As in the French Convention during the Revolution. It's Marsh that makes the pope. The terms used to describe the parties are different from those used in politics, but they function in the same way. Sometimes the pope emerges from the Marsh. He is the smallest common denominator from the two opposite clans. They will accept him if they can't get one of theirs to be elected. From time to time, he comes from the left, more often from the right. When the moderates have joined one of the parties.

— What about the Curia of cardinals, are they as important as they say?

— Yes, there are 35 of them. Quite a homogenous group. They usually vote for the right, and for an Italian. To reinforce the political control of Italy. If they can't put an Italian conservative on Saint Peter's throne in the first round, they will make do with a moderate's representative. But, only an Italian, mind! One who will do what they want him to do.

— All this is not very pastoral, Vittorio laughed!

— Oh! If I were to serve you the ecclesiastical vocabulary brushed with honey, you wouldn't understand anything.

— And where do you stand?

— Oh, not a chance for me, thank God! We vote and, hop, back to Venice.

— Do you already know who you are going to vote for yet?

— Yes, but don't let it out, we're not allowed to tell. We are risking excommunication. In confidence, it will be for Lochscheider. He's a nice Brazilian, a friendly man and not dogmatic in the least. He's neither Italian nor European, he would open the windows and it would be of great help to the Church that is to set in its ways. He could continue with John XXIII's line of thinking; he disappeared too soon.

— You're slightly revolutionary!

— No, just evolutionary, Luciani laughed out loud. Just think of simple but essential subjects such as birth control, married priests, how to fit women in the Church or the Vatican's wealth accumulation. These are questions which can easily be resolved with common sense and compassion. A duster could be very useful in this decrepit place.

— I do hope you will get elected with all these ideas.

— Don't worry, you can sleep tight. No chance of me falling into all this. What about some food? Can you take me to one of your favorite restaurants?

— I'm meeting Nancy there at one o'clock. Do you mind if the three of us have lunch together?

— Fine. I'll just put on something more discreet. And I'll be there. I'm looking forward to seeing her again.

— See you soon.

Saturday August 26 — the Vatican

Two days later, on the evening of August 26th, the protodeacon cardinal appeared on the balcony of Saint Peter's Basilica. During more than an hour, black, white or gray smoke had been seen from the chimney. Inside the Sistine Chapel, the cardinals were throwing their notes in the fire. They were creating black smoke, blending with the white smoke being emitted by the cardinal in charge.

He was shouting:

— But stop, godd..., in Heaven's name!

But while he was having a go at one of them, another would be getting rid of his notes into the stove, behind his back.

The radio journalists were trying to work it out.

— In canon law, what does the alternating of white and black smoke mean when mixed with gray?

— Probably a Curia novelty. To signal that no new pope has been chosen yet. But that the Conclave has almost hit the target.

— Quite Thierry. The Church will never stop amazing us with its innovations, its ability to adapt. It's wonder…

— Excuse me, I've just been told that liturgical singing can be heard from the Sistine Chapel.

— Would that mean that the Cardinals are happy?

— Yes, and if they are, it means that a pope has been elected.

— Absolutely. But the smoke, I can't really see from here. Can you see it from where you stand?

— Yes, I can see it very well. It's perfectly clear: it's gray.

This is what had been going on for an hour on the world's radios when the protodeacon's figure appeared on the famous balcony. He adjusted and tapped the microphone, then proclaimed, "Habemus Papam!"

The clamor of the mob on the Vatican Square grew louder. Then Albino Luciani appeared, all dressed in white. He greeted the believers with a wide smile. Then he disappeared.

But the crowd cheered him so much that he had to come back, like in a theater.

Deeply moved, he was thinking: "How did I fall into such a sticky situation?"

He had had such an insane day. It was all wrapped into a single day. The previous day's vote had only been a first test-round. But today was a cavalry charge. The first vote, then the second and finally the last one. And there he was, Pope! He had oddly thought about the repairs to his Lancia 2000. Who would bring it back to Venice? He was distraught, as if he had crashed and burned.

He had heard, in a deep fog:

— Do you accept?

He mumbled:

— May God forgive you for what you've done to me.

The voice came back:

— Do you accept?

He heard himself answering:

— I accept.

How idiotic! But what else could he do? The sin of pride, to deny the Holy Spirit's call?

— What name will you choose?

— Mmmm, John. . . Paul. John Paul I.

The cardinals were stunned by this choice. A double-barrelled name! Furthermore, no Supreme Pontiff had actually chosen a new given name for centuries. They were hopping around, congratulating themselves: what an amazing innovation, what a fertile imagination, what up-to-date boldness, what a message with those two Apostles! When he had, in fact, only opted for the names of the last two popes. That's all it was, it didn't mean anything in particular.

In the second round, he came in second place behind Tisi, but without enough votes to risk being elected. He prayed while his colleagues were having a nap.

— Oh! Lord! Don't do that to me, turn away from me, go to hell!

But after his siesta, he was crushed by the third round as by a hippopotamus. He was really leading. As the votes got called out, he whispered,

— No, Lord, no Lord!

He turned towards his neighbors,

— Please don't do this to me, please!

Conservative Cardinal Tisi's score had collapsed, Luciani was given 68 votes.

"Come on, keep cool Albino! Let's see, 111 divided by 3 and multiplied by 2 makes 74. Plus one equals 75. Only 7 votes left before the disaster. What about lifting my cassock and showing my bum to the assembly, would that put them off?"

He didn't know what to do. He remained totally still on his bench. The fourth vote began.

"I can still refuse. But if I accept, I'll have to find a name. Oh God! Please help me, I've never thought of that. Let's see, John XXIII was a good man. John XXIV would be acceptable, it's simple. But all those figures: it's a bit dumb. We don't give children numbers: Sophie 1st, Sophie IInd, Sophie IIIrd. Gaspard 1st, Gaspard IInd, Gaspard IIIrd etc. What shambles in a family? I must innovate."

His name came up more and more.

"Quick, be quick, you don't have lots of time left! John made me Bishop, Paul Cardinal. John Paul. Funny name."

At that very minute, he finally smiled, relieved and amused by that craziness. They all thought he was happy with his imminent election.

— Results! declared the Camerlengo: Cardinal Luciani 99 votes. Elected.

The following morning, he woke up completely groggy in the pontifical apartment. After breakfast and a terrible coffee, he started calling his friends to seek comfort. It was the last time he would be able to talk as a mere human being and not as God's Representative on earth. He told one of them,

— I can't understand how I accepted. Last night I already regretted. But it was too late.

And to another one,

— Just see what's happening to me!

Monday August 28 – the Vatican

Vittorio Petri had mixed feelings. He was happy about the event, but he was losing his beloved Uncle. The day after the election he held back from contacting him. He could really imagine Albino in this maelstrom. But he had to speak to the pope. Not about their feelings. Nor about the Lancia.

On August 28th, he called the Secretariat of the Pontifical Council from his IOR internal number. Completely blocked. The pope was too busy, with a billion believers to cope with, just to see a simple Curia employee who pretended to be his nephew. And moreover, even if he were, he no longer had a family, his family now being the Catholics all over the world. Tired of this slop, he gave up after two unsuccessful attempts.

Tuesday August 29 - the Vatican

On August 29th, the new pope called him. Would he come and share dinner in the pontifical apartment? They had a nice time, full of warmth, as if Albino's status hadn't changed.

— How am I to address you now, Uncle? Holy Father?

— Just as before, but try to avoid familiarity when if public. The Curia scrutinizes civility. Thousands of people are looking after me. I'm in the Vatican's net. I have already been forbidden to go for a walk in town, in my parish.

— Oh, the pope can be denied …?

— Well, they tell me it's impossible. It would start riots! It's like with the sedan chair. That thing where the pope sits, carried by men and exhibited in the crowd. I don't want it. Such a show of strength for trifles! At least I managed not to wear the three-story pie-shaped tiara. And to replace the crowning ceremony by a simple mass. Six hours saved. And symbolism closer to its origins.

— Centuries ago, well no, just five days ago you told me that you found the Church too wealthy.

— Of course, I remember.

— Does John Paul I agree on that point with Albino Luciani?

— Of course, what are you getting at?

— When we were cycling in Venice, you reminded me that I was held to professional secrecy. Well, I no longer am. I must tell the Chef what is cooking in his pots.

— Compelling logic. You're scaring me. I'm listening.

Vittorio explained how the Church's financial institutions operated, led by IOR. The Vatican was an organized crime money laundering machine. With sublaunderettes. The main one was Ambrosiano Bank, controlled by Roberto Calvi. He replaced Michele Sindona in 1974 as Cosa Nostra's banker when Sindona fled to the United States. Archbishop Paul Marcinkus, then IOR's Director and a few Vatican accomplices helped the machinery to operate at full capacity. Vittorio outlined this complex trafficking process to the pope.

— Why did you stay, he asked his nephew? Hadn't I recommended you walked away if you spotted dirty dealings?

— I only recently understood the whole mechanism. It was well disguised! I did have suspicions before. Now I'm certain of it. It's dangerous to get involved. The rush of adrenaline makes me want to know more. It's such a huge deal! Paul VI was old and sick. Without wishing him dead — or let's say hoping for it as he covered everything up – I must admit I was hoping for a new pope who wouldn't accept all this, any longer. In whom I could have confided without risking being found drowned in the Tiber. I would never have guessed it could be you. We are so close to the Mafia, which doesn't have a good record on human rights. I've informed you, but be very prudent. Don't talk to anyone about it. You know nothing, you say nothing. If you take a decision, prepare your dismissals and hit them altogether, all at once. Excuse me, I'm losing my temper. You didn't ask me for advice. But I love you, so here it is. Take care, Uncle. If they get hold of information, they won't hold back.

Thursday August 31 — the Vatican

Albino Luciani was a simple man, but with a strong religious experience. Once the initial shock of the election passed, he told himself once you pop, you can't stop. He kept pinching himself, he really was the pope. Why not benefit from it by conveying his favorite beliefs? As he would be heard by the whole world and not only by a half-empty church, he wouldn't hold back.

Giovanni-Paolo 1st was too long for the Italians. They would call him Gianpaolo, which he found so pleasant, he used it for his signature. The State Secretary brought him the papers to ratify, imploring him just to sign them correctly. Which he ended up doing, to make him happy.

He had always been oddly dressed in his public life: priest, bishop, archbishop, cardinal. He was used to this. The color of the cassock didn't change much. Very relaxed, he gave his keynote addresses successfully, press conferences, diplomatic corps addresses, inauguration masses, Saturday Angelus and Wednesday general audience.

But the Curia's apparatchiks were watching. The Holy Father's speeches were censured. Anything published had been filtered by the Curia. If Gianpaolo had been, funny, spontaneous or just himself, it would not be apparent as the written transcriptions were fake. To trap him, the Osservatore Romano published that the pope was against birth control, whereas he supported it. Making this a first symbolic murder.

Alessa Lombardi had attended the press conference for journalists from around the world. Like her colleagues, she had been seduced by the spontaneity and simplicity of the new pope. But three days later, intrigued, she wrote in her notebook:

« Strange, Gianpaolo seemed to be for birth control and the Osservatore Romano reports exactly the opposite! Clear it up. Interview this new pope. »

The revelations of the pope's nephew required financial reform. How could this be accomplished without unleashing the Octopus? Albino Luciani mixed this topic with others. It was normal to overview the situation. One does it for an apartment. He asked Cardinal State Secretary Villot to carry out audits on religious and financial matters.

Villot was accorded a fortnight to submit his projects. One month for the intermediate audits and three months for the final ones. Villot objected tooth and nail, one excuse after another, le pope remained inflexible.

The news of his determination to reform and get rid of abuses spread at great speed. Elio Cighi had his informers in the Vatican: high prelate members of his P2 lodge. He was very close to Calvi and Marcinkus. This bloody new pope was going to spoil the laundering machine, for sure. It was imperative to stop him before he did more damage. With the good will of the Palermo godfather Gino Dalo, their devout followers decided that an unbalanced anti-papist would have it in for him. This rare bird would be easy to find amongst the Mafia grunts. They had promised to obey their bosses once and for all. There was no choice. They just had to organize the operation's details.

Self-assured, Cighi started to gather his networks.

— Your Eminence, they say Giovanni-Paolo 1st suffers from very poor health, poor man. If he came to die, who would you see as a new pope? One never knows. No need to be caught short.

The noose was tightening around Luciani's neck.

Friday September 1 – Rome

Nancy Jones entered briskly at the United States Embassy in Rome. On the 5th floor, her NSA team was bunkered, featuring a top-of-the-line security gate. The Ambassador himself didn't even have access. No more than the CIA members also bunkering in the other wing.

She was the diplomatic representation scientific attaché, as well as a university lecturer.

— Hi, my friends, she said entering the place that looked more like a space shuttle than an office.

— Anything new?

One of her colleagues handed over a decoded transcription. He was passing the tapes through a decoder. Nancy had programmed it. It was the decoder of Crypto AG, a Swiss company that inspired confidence. Since 1955, these encoding machines were fitted with a back door set by the American secret services under Crypto AG's orders. The back door was updated according to new technological developments. About a hundred countries were spied on in this way. Private individuals had also started working on Crypto AG machines communicating by radio waves, with which they were delighted.

This is what the recording looked like before the decryption:

"sfjaàq230'98 534

"32POP8234NéE1fdjkdé1§éà$a.asdfnsdéqwklefms„mgp oréLKJ4/=cnsleksapjjgeéà23'045asdenmaélsgpww0et8m vleàqélèpèqpwoet'038'08032948MJlsejdg'34058élksjglyél xknmckklfàqlj90e58'2'309648<s^'"   1 sgkjmcmqè.12'49…" Etc., etc.

And, after decoding, it looked like this:

— …. *Wednesday, September 6th, 10 a.m., Nervi Hall, weekly general audience. A sniper. A second one backing him. A third one for exfiltration if necessary. But the last two are instructed not to move and to dump number one. He's sacrificed for a good cause, but doesn't know this, of course.*

— *Can your sniper keep his nerve?*

— *Yes, he is cold-blooded. He is intelligent and will not be put off by cops. He'll play the game*

— *Perfect. Thanks to the plan and the information. If he gets caught alive, he'll make them believe he's an unbalanced anti-papist, is that it?*

— *Absolutely. And if he shifts from this version, his life in prison will be short.*

— *Perfect.*

Nancy worked in her office all morning. That conversation had been intercepted the previous day between the *mafioso* godfather Gino Dalo in Palermo and Elio Cighi, head of the P2 lodge who was in Buenos Aires. She knew who the second one was. For the first one, she consulted the computer linked by protected cable to the Head of NSA in Maryland.

- *Gino Dalo*
- *Born September 30, 1931*
- *Sicilian Mafioso*
- *Called Cosa Nostra Cashier, as heavily involved in whitewashing*
- *Godfather since 1962*
- *Member of the Provincial Commission, then of Cupola. He often goes to Rome.*

● *Linked with neo-fascists, politicians, Italian secret service members, prelates and bankers.*

She had visited Nervi Hall at the Vatican. Wednesday's general audience was given by the pope to a crowd of believers in the huge auditorium. An ideal location to shoot him on the Sedia gestatoria, his sedan chair. On August 30th, for the first time, he had refused to use it and opted to go on foot. Nancy had read about this in the morning papers, which were very fond of this new casual style. But the Curia had insisted. If the pope was carried, the people would see him. Otherwise not. He had given in. This was the gossip found in the newspapers.

On Wednesday 6th, he would be sitting on this contraption. The perfect target.

At 3 p.m., she called the NSA Manager for Maryland, Paul Burbon. It was 9 a.m. on the East Coast. A very short exchange.

— Hello Paul.

— Hello Nancy.

— Please take this down?

— Yes.

— On Wednesday 6th September at 10 o'clock, Rome time; there will be an attempt on the pope's life, during the weekly general audience in the Nervi Hall. He will be clearly visible, either on the podium or carried in his sedan chair, well above the crowds' heads. It's a modern hall. It can take up to 6,000 people. There will be a sniper. Two accomplices will be there to support him or to help him escape. But they won't. The sniper will be left behind. It's the Sicilian mafia's godfather, Gino Dalo, who is organizing the party. The mentor is Elio Cighi of Lodge P2, currently hiding in Buenos Aires. You can see their files in the Central machine.

— Thank you, Nancy. It's clear. I reckon it's impossible for the Swiss Guards to check out the faithful. I presume there's no security checkpoint.

— None. It's an open house day.

— I'll warn the President. And advise him to alert the Pope. Do you know the reason?

— The new Pope is known not to conform and to reform. My friend is his nephew. I hear things. And the traffickers and receivers aren't too happy: we've been listening to them and their tricks for months.

— OK. Thank you. And what about the mafia/CIA collusion that was worrying about the President? Nothing's happened yet?

— Nothing yet. It's quiet on that front. We've been listening for 2 years. Old data if you want my opinion. You can reassure the president. At any rate according to what you can hear in Rome.

Friday 1 – Washington

Five minutes later, the NSA Director called President Jimmy Carter's Cabinet Secretary.

— Hi Jack, is the president in Washington now?

— Yes.

— I need to see him today.

— Is 4 p.m. OK?

— Any chance of seeing him before lunch?

— Let's see. I'll shift this one, postpone the French ambassador, quarter past eleven?

— Thank you, Jack. See you later.

President Carter welcomed the NSA Director at the White House Oval Office.

— Hi Paul. Make yourself comfortable. Why are you here?

They sat facing each other on the famous sofas.

— Thank you for having me here, Mr. President.

— I'm listening to you.

After the information was given by the NSA Director,

— What would you advise me to do, Carter asked?

— To call the pope today. There's very little time, and the Vatican is like a sieve.

— I will. Anything else?

— Yes. His private apartment, twenty rooms. They may be tapped. Above all, his office and his telephone. You'll call him on a protected line. Safer. But could you try to make him understand that risk, at the beginning of the conversation? And get him not to talk. You should be the only one to speak and get him not to answer other than by one-word responses. You could give him all the details about the planned attack; and advise him to protect his apartment from all kinds of tapping. You can send him a specialist. Keep me informed if he agrees. I'll send him someone the same day.

— Ha, ha! cried out the President. You're making a spy of me! I love it! It's a change from my peanut plantation in Georgia. Anything else Paul?

— The CIA is untroubled by the mafia nowadays. Nothing new in Rome. It's calm. It's lost in history.

— Perfect. But bearing in mind today's scoop, keep maintaining Rome at a high alert level. And congratulate them on my behalf!

— I shall do so. Thank you, Mr. President.

Friday 1 – the Vatican

Father Magee, one of the pope's secretaries, told him the United States President was online.

— Pass him on in my office.

Carter did what the NSA Director had advised. Gianpaolo played the game and thanked the president. If a microphone had been in the room, this is what it would have transmitted over five minutes:

— Yes, . . . yes, . . . yes, . . no, . . . absolutely clear, . . thank you, understood, ... good,.... willingly . . ., yes, . . Have a good day, . . thank you, . . . goodbye.

The pope had managed to control his emotions during his conversation with President Carter. But as soon as he put down the phone, they overwhelmed him. This palace was a death trap. Jesus Christ's message of goodness and charity had been thrown in the bin. He was outraged. And he was frightened.

He asked not to be disturbed. He prayed for a long time. This helped calm him down. He came to his senses again. He was only the next one on the long list of deadly attacks in the last ten years. Why would this pope have been better protected than any other? But he didn't want to end as Aldo Moro did. He wanted to live. Just simply live.

He told Jesus in his prayer that he was only a humble sinner. I don't have your strength to give up my life, the way you did. I can't sacrifice myself. I'd like to live a little longer before hoping to enter your Kingdom.

He suddenly remembered the information the Camerlengo had given him on the evening of his election. There was a casket in the safe that only the pope was allowed to open. With information for him. He had forgotten this. These medieval gadgets didn't really interest him. But, as things stood, it could be worth giving it a glance. He opened the safe, then the casket. It was equipped with a clever mechanism whose instructions were hidden in an envelope sealed in the old-fashioned way. With Paul VI's seal, which had been destroyed when he died. The envelope was very obviously laid in the box. The red seal was untouched. He broke it and opened the envelope. He then set off the casket's device. There he found another sealed document with the plans of the secret passages inside the Vatican, as well as those leading outside the Vatican. He memorized the main ones. Tried one of them. It was in his library. A section of the wall swiveled open onto a dark corridor. He started to walk down it, blocking open the panel behind him with a piece of furniture.

"You never know with this stuff. In my childhood books, the passage always closes, and you get stuck." But this wasn't the case. After twenty meters, a portion of the wall swiveled with a simple thrust on a stone block.

"Oh, oh! Clever. You just have to push when it's ajar."

He pushed. He was outside. In front of him, a passage at the top of a strong wall about fifteen meters high. The clearly very old stone pathway was narrow and pointed straight ahead towards Castel San Angelo, on the bank of the Tiber. It looked like a medieval fortress walkway.

Bordered by high walls on each side. One could walk there without being seen.

"The former popes must also have been in danger, to build such escape tracks. With, in addition, the underground paths under the Sistine Chapel and from the Byzantine Basilica. Why not use those archaic means to fool my enemies?"

Albino Luciani felt better. He had tools and a project.

He went back to the library, made a few notes, memorized the main plans, and put them all back with envelopes sealed with his seal. It was getting late. He went to have dinner. From the dining room, he called his nephew Vittorio to invite him the following evening, September 2. After a quick meal, he asked the staff not to disturb him until the next morning.

— I'm here for no-one, no visit, no telephone, no service, good night.

He then retired and tested his plan. He went for a walk via the Passeto di Borgo, as it was called on the ancient diagram, above Rome to the Castel San Angelo and back. Two kilometers. Without being noticed. He was kept from prying eyes thanks to the high walls. He went to bed with his mind completely at rest.

"Tomorrow, let's explore the other bit of the passage; a little incognito walk through town."

He fell asleep dreaming of secret and mysterious getaways, having fun at the idea that this adult pope felt so close to his childhood daydreaming.

Saturday 2 – Rome

He received his nephew the following evening and showed him these words scribbled on a piece of paper:

- there are microphones
- let's not talk about it
- let's only refer to insignificant general matters
- we'll eat quickly
- then we'll vanish into the library
- to meditate
- I requested not to be disturbed until tomorrow
- You'll follow me without speaking

They withdrew after the meal, which didn't surprise the staff who had attended the previous pope. Paul VI sometimes left with a young priest. To pray.

Albino Luciani left his nephew alone for a moment and came back dressed in his jeans, a short-sleeved shirt, trainers and baseball cap. A wall of the library swiveled silently, leading to a passage.

They went in. The wall closed behind them. It wasn't completely dark in the tunnel. Tiny openings at the top of the walls let in a bit of light and fresh air.

— Mind where you step, it's messy, whispered the pope. My predecessors didn't clean up very often!

They moved on almost fifteen meters. Another panel, of stone this time, swiveled. It looked as though they were on oiled hinges. They were set on the outside, at the level of the third story of the papal palace. On the wall walk of a castle. But, instead of being circular, it went straight ahead. It was still daytime. They walked in single file along this narrow path strewn with stuff many centuries had dumped there. They stepped over loads of dust, a cat and a kite's carcasses. Vittorio was amazed to glimpse the massive outlines of Castello San Angelo in the distance. The hustle and bustle of the city rose towards them. Children's screams, engines humming, car horns.

After walking one kilometer without talking, they came up to the castle's northwest bastion. Vittorio thought they were going to go back after this open walk. But no. His uncle pushed on two places in the wall. An opening appeared in the wall. Both companions were indoors, in front of a spiral staircase. Another passage went straight on. Albino signaled to go down the steps. Passing a postern, they found themselves in the gardens with a bird's-eye view on the ancient moats. They walked down a path towards a modest town wall; it was of a later construction, surrounded by thick vegetation. A door was hidden by two chicanes. Strolling through a grassy stretch, they came to Piazza Pia. They crossed the Tiber on Saint Angelo's bridge amongst the tourists. The Vatican's prisoner loved walking incognito in the indifferent crowd. They went right up to the Trevi Fountain, via Piazza Navona and the Pantheon.

— I must call your mom now. I'll explain this later, said Albino. Just one question: can you take three or four days off as from Tuesday evening?

— Yes, I have a few extra hours owed to me.

— And could you wait for me, with your little Fiat in Piazza Pia?

— Yes.

— And would you be willing to take me incognito to Cortina d'Ampezzo?

— Yes.

— Thank you. Here is a telephone booth. Whoops! No coins! I'm a misfit already, he laughed!

Vittorio gave him the change. Albino called his sister Nina. Could she put them up, Vittorio and himself for three nights as from the 5th or the 6th? Without telling anyone. He would explain everything when he got there. Above all, not to tell anyone. Stunned and astonished, she promised. He added:

— Listen Nina, I need a spiritual retreat after all this. I must get away from the papal pomp for a few days and spend time with my loved ones. No journalist or cardinal on my back. I'm sure you can understand, living in such a quiet life. I'm also yearning for this. I need your help. I feel trapped everywhere else.

Nina was reassured.

— Can I talk about it to Ettore?

— To your husband, yes. By no one else. He too must keep quiet as the grave. Promise, little sister?

— Promised, promised. Don't worry. Come over, my dear brother. We're looking forward to seeing you both.

The evening was quite mild, sitting on a terrace, on the Piazza Navona. Normal people were peacefully strolling along.

— It feels good here, sighed the pope, his baseball cap on his head.

Vittorio roared with laughter. Sharing these happy moments, Albino told his nephew what had happened.

— Was our phone conversation listened to?

— Perhaps, my reforms scare some of them. President Carter is sending a specialist to check for microphones. And protect me from tapping. He'll call me on my direct line and will introduce himself as a controller of the electrical devices. On Tuesday evening, I will arrive between eight thirty and nine thirty. We could take turns at the wheel, up to Cortina. If it's too tiring, we could stop overnight in Bologna.

— Perfect.

— I'll tell Villot to cancel at 8 o'clock on Wednesday the 10 o'clock audience. It won't come as a surprise to anyone as, when the pope is away or feeling unwell, it's the usual thing to do. Except for the killers. They will understand that their plan has been uncovered. We shall have to expect a counterattack. Very distressing to be the mafia's target.

After watching lovers throwing coins in the Trevi fountain, they strolled back, forgetting the threat for a moment.

Sunday 3 – the Vatican

At 8 o'clock, on Sunday morning, his private line rang. It was the expert promised by President Carter. He arrived at 9 o'clock, at 11 o'clock it was all done. The major rooms were secured. He would come back each week for a check. It wouldn't cost anything, it was just a friendly hand.

At 11 o'clock, John Paul I asked his State Secretary to meet him at 2 o'clock in his Cabinet. Villot objected that it was the Lord's Day and his siesta time. The pope argued that they had a lot to do and that the Lord wouldn't mind.

At midday, Gianpaolo appeared at the window, for the Angelus public prayer.

At 1 o'clock, he had lunch on his own.

At 2 o'clock, he greeted Cardinal Villot, even more sullen than usual.

— Well, Your Eminence, are you with or against me, challenged the pope.

— But with you, Holy Father, with you, said Villot, flabbergasted by his bluntness.

— We've been working together for a week now and either you object to my propositions systematically or you simply say they are impossible.

— Well, Holy Father, your suggestions are so very different from those of your predecessor. As you are new in such a high position, I thought it was my duty to let you know. In order to let you make informed decisions.

— Thank you for your concern. I can understand it up to a point, being provincial with no experience of governing. You keep declaring, "The previous pope didn't do things this way, he wouldn't have done it that way." Let me tell you: it's the end of this. Paul VI is dead. The only thing you can do for him is to ask the Council of Elders for a beatification. Paul VI has nothing more to say in this world. I'm the pope today. Is it clear enough?

— It couldn't be clearer, Your Holiness. But if I may. . .

— Yes?

— You were elected by 99 voices out of 111. The Cardinals who voted for you, above all those of the Curia, would feel betrayed if you started reforms that don't match their wishes.

— I didn't woo anyone, I made no promises to anybody, I don't owe anything to anyone.

— But you are the pope, Holy Father.

— I didn't look for it. And you, being Camerlengo, know this better than anybody. I hesitated to say "I accept" when you asked me. You had to ask me twice. Let's not prevaricate. Yes, I said yes. I'm the pope. And the pope asks you once more, "are you with or against him?"

— With him.

— Good.

— Well. I asked you to remain my State secretary despite your age and your health, in order to help me sort things out. Thank you for having said yes. And as you are with me, please would you accept to stay with me till next year? And to submit your choice for three surrogates? We'll examine your pre-choices, and then I'll decide.

— I agree, Holy Father.

« Good, Luciani thought, I shook him up, but he seems to be staying on my side. He is so quiet! He shuts up like a clam. But something tells me that beneath his shell, he's a good guy. I must take the risk. In any case, I have no choice. Let's get started! »

— What's to follow is confidential, your Eminence. Strictly between you and me. No written note. No talking to anyone.

— All right, I'm listening.

— My apartment and my telephone line have been secured.

— Ah! You didn't tell me! Paul VI wouldn't have worried about tapping. He would have asked me.

The pope laughed.

— See, you can't help it, there you are again, Your Eminence! I, Gianpaolo 1ˢᵗ, I am concerned about tapping. And I, Gianpaolo 1ˢᵗ, don't pass everything through my Secretary of State. I sometimes happen to act for myself.

— I'm sorry dear Holy Father, I must recognize I have a crease in my cassock, said Villot with a smile.

— Can we get to the heart of the matter?

— Yes, yes, I won't interrupt again.

— Next Wednesday, September 6th at 10 o'clock, I will get shot. It will happen in the Nervi Hall during the general audience. I've unequivocally been told. It's a structured plot. I don't know the reason. My hopes for reform could have filtered through. I'm taking the following measures: on Tuesday evening I'll leave the Vatican incognito. Paul VI's sealed information will be useful. I can't tell you more. At 10 o'clock on Tuesday evening, you'll gather my personal team. You'll tell them that I'll be away for a few days, that they must keep it secret, and continue as usual. At 8 o'clock on Wednesday morning, you'll get Radio Vatican to announce that the 10 o'clock audience in the Nervi Hall is canceled. Without explanations. If you get asked questions, it will be "no comment" which will avoid the sin of lying. You'll manage the store the way you do so competently when the pope is away. For your own information, I'm going off for 3 to 4 days' spiritual retreat. I plan to be back during the night 8th to 9th. If you get your apartment and line secured, I'll try to call you. Otherwise, I won't call you. That's all. Any questions? Suggestions?

— No, it's quite clear, Holy Father. I'm wholly with you. Even if differences exist on apostolic matters, they mean nothing compared with what they are attempting against you. It's appalling. And I'm willing to see your tapping expert.

— Thank you for your support, Your Eminence. It's of great help. He'll be there tomorrow. He'll tell you he's there to check the electric features. It's free. Don't try to understand. God sometimes helps us. Remember. Not a word about all this to anyone.

THE ZUGZWANG

September 5 - 8, 1978

Tuesday 5

It was 1 a.m., they had been driving for four hours in Vittorio's Fiat. In the Venetia, the former archbishop of Venice's Lancia 2000 was too well known.

— Are we spending the night in Bologna, or shall we carry on? He asked Vittorio, who was driving.

— I'm OK, what about you?

— Me too, and I'm keen to get to Cortina. We're halfway. Shall I take over?

— In Padua, is that OK?

— Yes, said Albino, handing the driver a drink in the thermos mug. I'll relax till then.

Wednesday 6 - Cortina

At 6 a.m., it was already daylight when they stopped outside Nina and Ettore's. They would have liked to bring something to them, but everything was still shut. Ettore and Nina would have enjoyed a hard cheese from the Latteria Perenzin from San Pedro di Feletto, the best in the area. It was heavenly served with a Prosecco. But circumstances were unusual. After the greeting, having not seen each other since the conclave, they settled down.

Albino told them about the election, without disclosing numbers which would mean excommunication. But as he was in power, he could let some information slip without having to excommunicate himself. He spoke of his hesitation, of his misgivings at not saying no, of the strange unfolding of events and his sudden change of status. Nina kept crossing herself, Ettore was mocking her. Then Albino talked about the luxurious straitjacket of life at the Vatican. The only exercise he could take was to walk around the thousands of rooms at the palace. But this pope, who had turned up out of the blue, was a nuisance. He had just received secure information that he was going to be shot at that very day, during the general audition at 10 a.m. Nina signed herself again, saying a prayer under her breath. Ettore had stopped mocking her, and almost signed himself, too.

— That's why we have taken shelter with you, empty-handed but with heavy hearts.

— We need to be very discreet about Uncle Albino being here. The pope having fun, in jeans and baseball cap, you can just imagine the crowd of reporters! Let alone those who want to kill him.

They would stay for two nights then set off for Rome.

— I can't stay away any longer. Three days is already a great feat, smiled Albino. I am so looking forward to staying with you for these three days, which will do me a power of good after all these emotions. Up in the mountains, I will be neither pope nor cardinal.

They had a wash, slept a little, had lunch together, took a siesta and set off on the local footpaths before dinner. Nina had said:

— We will not go with you; we are too well known here. Ettore and I will not change anything to our usual routine so as not to draw attention to us. I'll keep the shop open, 10–12/3–5. And I will cook up some nice dishes of you. Ettore, are you happy to go to the shops and the café as usual? You hear more there than on the radio. We will soon know if something's up. Vittorio, and you in particular, Albino, come and go through the old pigsty. Vittorio, you can leave your Fiat outside the house. You are visiting us, it's natural, as a son.

Wednesday 6

On Wednesday 6 September, Elio Cighi, the venerable from Lodge P2, was glued to the radio. He had switched it on at 9:50. Nothing at 10:15, still nothing at 10:30. The shooter must be biding his time. He kept channel switching. There was not mention of the expected catastrophe on RAI. Less still on Vatican radio. He had missed the 8 a.m. bulletin. He didn't want to call his contacts now. After the attack, it would seem suspect. He kept quiet but was struggling to keep so.

Gino Dalo, the godfather who was leading the operation was also listening to broadcasts. At 10:30, one of his deputies called him. The audience had not taken place. The Vatican had given no reason. Dalo made a few calls. There were no comments from the Vatican. He called Cighi. He would find out under a different pretext. But not straightaway. Not before tomorrow. Gino Dalo was a particularly angry man and he was enraged. But he was also smart. He decided to wait. Cighi knew what he was doing.

Thursday 7 - Rome

The pope's escape had been kept well hidden by the secretary of State. Cighi tried to know more but he only found out what Villot was letting out: with whispers and without telling anyone, His Holiness was unwell. Nothing serious, a cold which confined him to his bedroom. His doctor hid behind confidentiality, along with reporters,

Staying calm, the Venerable and the godfather considered the next move. Thinking about it, they agreed that a shooting, even coming from a crazy anti-papist, wasn't sufficiently discreet to get rid of a pope. Many wouldn't believe it and that would create suspicions forever. There was nothing to be gained by shocked conservative Catholics leaving P2 and Cosa Nostra. They had to think of something else. A natural death was ideal. But John Paul was in great shape. What could one do? The thought of good old poison came up. One could engineer and simulate an ordinary death, without autopsy. The Secretary of State could be approached to avoid it. The plotters had a plan. They just had to work on the details. Thursday 7 ended in peace and quiet.

Wednesday 6 - Rome

Meanwhile, the sniper was frustrated. And concerned. He had to kill the pope. But his sermon had been canceled. He had also received orders not to contact his leaders. He was supposed to be mad, a loose cannon. He was alone. If he failed, the organization would show him and his family no mercy. But if he succeeded, he and his family would never know poverty again. He would be in jail or in a psychiatric hospital with all the comforts that went with men of honor. He absolutely had to kill the pope.

On the night from 6 to 7, he was watching the pontifical apartments with binoculars. He saw no sign of life. The pope wasn't ill. He was not at the Vatican. At Castel Gondolfo? On the morning of the 7, he traveled there. The official flag, which indicated the pope was in residence, wasn't flying. So where was he? He had read in a magazine after the election that the pope came from the Canale d'Agordo, a hole in the northern Pre-Alps. Perhaps he was visiting his family? Why not, after all? He was a man like any other, this guy.

The killer arrived at Canale d'Agordo on Thursday 7. He had a chat with a waitress in a restaurant and he had no trouble getting her to spill the beans. The entire village was talking about their local celebrity. It was easy to talk about him. His sister lived in a nearby valley, at Cortina d'Ampezzo, the ski resort; the siblings were very close. She had a souvenir shop. They even gave him its name. On the evening of 7, he was in Cortina and he knew where to find the sister. He watched the household. After dark, he could see the comings and goings of several people, who went to bed late. There was an air of festivity, of conviviality. He knew about this, being a Sicilian himself. He wasn't a sentimental killer, no, just an ordinary one, it was his job. Like so many others. He mustn't ask himself questions about his work. It wasn't good for him. He was a soldier. As soldiers, he did as he was told. He killed. Without cruelty. Simple. Technical. Same as abattoir employees who were no worse than those who planted tomatoes.

Wednesday 6 - Cortina

While he was at Cortina d'Ampezzo, the pope, now Albino Luciani, was spending happy moments with his family. They swapped news. What was he doing, what was she up to? They were proud of Albino's first cousin, Aldo Bonassoli, a well-known scientist. In their youth, Albino and Aldo had enjoyed many leisurely and sporting activities together, along with their parents who were siblings. They got on so well that they often spent holidays together. The numerous cousins loved to meet up and play. Eight years older than Aldo, Albino was like an older brother. At that blessed time, Aldo, the scientist was still little Aldino.

Vittorio Petri was 20 years younger than Aldo Bonassoli. He was the next generation. But they had often met up at big family gatherings, for Aldo was also his mother Nina's first cousin. Vittorio's sister had seen him recently. Aldo had also made important scientific breakthroughs. He worked for a big French oil producer, he traveled a lot. He still had a workshop in Lurano, near Bergamo, which he liked to go back to whenever he could. And above all, he was still a nice, extrovert and optimistic chap. It was a pleasure to come across him.

Thursday 7 - Cortina

On Thursday, Albino and Vittorio had been deep in the mountains, avoiding cable cars and restaurants. They dreaded what might happen after this restful break. Cosa Nostra wouldn't give up. They were scared. What could they do? Ask the Americans for protection? Unrealistic. Demand protection from Italy? Poisoned by the Octopus. Give up the reform of the finances of the Vatican? That would make me an accomplice. And yet, John Paul I thought, Paul VI had been mixed up with this. These thoughts were troubling them as they contemplated the magnificent panorama of the Dolomites. Such beauty calmed them. As did the salami and small bottle of vino rosso, Nina had packed into their bags.

That evening, Albino and Vittorio played chess. Ettore and Nina watched their game to the end. All were sipping coffee and grappa. It was Albino's turn. But he was going to lose, lose no matter what he did. He couldn't pass his turn. That was the rule.

— It's a zugzwang, he said. The move will be bad in any case. It's exactly the situation I am in. I am so happy here, with you, with people I love, in my beloved mountains. If only time could stop. But I'm stuck. I am returning tomorrow to the Vatican's trap. Chess sometimes mimics real life.

He played and lost.

In the middle of the night, the dog, asleep at Nina's feet, moaned. Nina understood the language of the Labrador. A human being was very close to the house. Alert and very worried about the danger her brother was in, she got up soundlessly and without putting on the light. She slipped into the room where Albino and Vittorio were asleep, woke them up, signaled to them to get dressed and to escape through the pigsty. Outside, they went through a narrow passage between two buildings.

At that moment the killer entered the house. The dog jumped on him. Stunned, he fired a shot. The Labrador writhed around on the ground for a few seconds then kept still. All this had happened with little noise as he had a silencer. He kept Ettore and Nina under threat with his weapon and asked where the Pope was.

— The Pope, are you mad? There is no pope here! This is not the Vatican! Nina replied.

The killer threw her to the ground, stuck his gun in her mouth and spoke coldly to Ettore:

— If you don't tell me within three seconds where the pope is hiding, I know he's around, I kill your wife, one, two, thr. . .

— He just left by the back door, squeaked Ettore.

At that moment, they heard the Fiat start.

The killer fled outside and got into his car in hot pursuit.

Vittorio was driving, Albino at his side. They saw the headlights in the rearview mirror. Vittorio accelerated as much as he could.

— I have an escape plan, said Albino.

— Go on!

— Listen carefully and do as I say. I'm your navigator, like in a rally.

The tires were squeaking on the dry road. Theirs were the only cars around at this late hour. At a crossroad the

Fiat suddenly left the main road and slipped into a side road. Both cars were driving fast. The road started to climb, with more and more bends and sharp corners, sometimes hairpin bends. They were in second gear now, the car nearly stalling.

— Keep some speed! We mustn't go into the first! We'll be shot at close range, advised Albino.

But oddly, when the pursuing car came close, they were not being shot at. But there was no time to figure this out. They had reached a plateau. The dirt track wound its way through a forest planted with larch trees. It now sloped gently downhill. It was no longer a track, but the space between the trees and the level ground made it look like one. Vittorio could now drive much faster than when going uphill. Suddenly, he braked sharply, hitting the pedal. The Fiat skidded on the needle floor then, almost at a standstill, took a right angle to the left. Stunned by this maneuver, the other car was too slow to react. It overtook them and plunged into the sheer void. After a few seconds, they heard in the distance a dull, double explosion.

— You saved our lives, gasped Vittorio, his forehead on the wheel.

— Without your driving, we were done for. I knew you knew your surroundings and that you would be able to use them. You saved us.

— No, it was you, with your idea.

— Did you see what I did, me, a priest! I'm not proud. We couldn't let ourselves be slaughtered.

They went down the mountain, more steadily this time.

— During the fascist era, said Albino, and during the war, we saw many horrors. We developed tactics of avoidance to stay alive. Initially to avoid fascist black shirts, then German SS. But I had never been directly involved as I was tonight. It's scary having to kill to survive. And it happens so quickly there is no time to consider the pros and cons.

It must have been around 2 a.m. In their flight they had not taken their watches. They parked away from the house and watched it for about twenty minutes. All the lights were out in the neighborhood, except Nina and Ettore's. Occasionally a shadow went past a lit window. There was no activity around. They waited a long time. The night was warm, even at this altitude. Finally, they took a chance and walked quietly through the pigsty.

Nina and Ettore were mourning their bitch who appeared to be sleeping, stretched out as she did when she felt too hot. Imminent danger seemed to have gone. They told each other what had happened, the death of the Labrador, the threat to Nina, the race, the crash into the void. The killer seemed to be on his own. When he got into the car for the chase, Ettore had seen him from the window, while Nina was lying on the floor. He had gotten in on the driver's side.

After a few hours' rest during which no-one was able to sleep, Albino and Vittorio decided to return to Rome. Cortina wasn't safe.

Nina and Ettore were not in much danger: the killer was only after the pope. He had said so. The Labrador's death was a sad accident. To be extra careful, Nina and Ettore would take a trip all the same.

So, the killer was on his own. It was odd and illogical. But what did this peaceful family know about the ways of gangsters? Had they underestimated their ability to resist, their craftiness?

They decided not to tell the police. They were not quite sure why. They felt they would be unable to defend Albino. Maybe the police were infiltrated. Under fascism, which they had all lived through except Vittorio, power was synonymous with danger.

Ettore and Nona buried the dog in the garden. They would tell neighbors, puzzled not to see her any longer, that she had died a natural death.

THE IDEA

September 9 - 18, 1978

Friday 8 - the Vatican

At 4:30 a.m., sister Vincenza brought the first coffee pot into the office. Then she knocked on Gianpaolo's door to wake him.

— Good morning, Holy Father.

He trusted her. They had worked together for twenty years and had always gotten on famously. After prayers, which he needed more than usual, Luciani had breakfast wearing his white cassock. She then gave Father Magee, one of his secretaries, who slept on the next floor, permission to see the pope.

— Good morning, Holy Father, have you recovered?

— Good morning, Father Magee, he said with a smile, if you were asked the question, what would you say after looking at me?

— Hem, that you are fully fit.

— There you are, you have your answer. So, what is the news? Today's folders? What is my schedule?

Saturday 9 - Washington

At 2 p.m., the President of the United States, Jimmy Carter called John Paul I on his secure direct line, which had been set up by the specialist.

Carter told him that an assassination attempt was in the wind. With poison this time. On a specific day, in his evening chamomile, to be carried out by the Sicilian mafia with internal accomplices at the heart of the Italian state and the Vatican. The type of poison and the date were not yet known. The conspirators had to settle some final details. The president said he would call the moment he knew more. He wished him good luck.

Saturday 9 - the Vatican

This time, the shock hit Luciani hard. He was only just getting over the double murder attempt and already... all the alternatives were running through his head. None was good. All had pitfalls, inconvenience or worse, dangers.

He was in a mousetrap, like some popes from the Middle Ages and the Renaissance.

To step down? It had not happened in centuries. The pope was not a head of state like any other. And it would not be sufficient to stop the Octopus. They would want to finish the job, to prevent things turning against them. There was a contract on his head, that is what it was called, Vittorio had explained. Cosa Nostra never let their prey run. Unless it was to collaborate with them. Better die. If he stepped down, he would be a kind of honorary pope. With no power to change anything, but with the inconvenience of appearances. A survival trophy. No thank you, I'd rather fucking die! "Oh sorry, God, it just slipped out!" "Don't worry, my son, pray and you will find the answer", said a gentle inner voice.

Which he did, at length. He forgot his siesta as he had during the election.

After praying, Albino Luciani started to see things more clearly. To stand down was out of the question. To stay as pope would mean to hang out on death row. He was 65, fit and still had interesting things to get on with life. To go back to being the archbishop of Venice was just as unrealistic and dangerous.

"As a priest, I did not vow anything other than celibacy and obedience to my bishop. At my age, celibacy is not a problem. As to obeying the bishop... as God's deputy on earth, God is my bishop now. He simply needs to allow me to give up being his deputy."

He prayed some more:

— Lord, you who know everything, you know better than anyone that I have sought neither wealth nor glory. I am only a poor sinner who is scared of dying. Free me, I beg you, of these chains which are too heavy for me.

He also remembered some of his Jesuit professors' teachings and God finally gave him absolution.

— I will obey you, God, he said, just as his old predecessor Moses had said on Mount Sinai, burning with volcanic fumaroles.

Now he knew where he wanted to go. But he had no idea how to get there.

Sunday 10 - the Vatican

On Sunday September 10, the antenna of the NSA at the US embassy was still listening whilst John Paul I was leading the Angelus prayer from the window. It was decorated with a piece of white cloth bearing his coat of arms.

All was quiet at the Vatican. And yet.

In the afternoon, Vittorio Petri came to find him. The pope told him of the American president's phone call.

Luciano was now determined to leave his post, without dying and without stepping down.

— That's the aim, my dear nephew, can you see a way to get there?

Vittorio thought for a while. Then he suggested that Albino Luciani disappeared from the pontifical palace, as he had done successfully twice before. But this time, it would be forever. Simply. The pope would have disappeared. People would think what they wanted. Some would think the Holy Spirit had had a hand in this, others would put forward more straightforward theories. Everyone to his beliefs.

— And thinking further ahead? If I were officially dead, it would eliminate any risky guesses. And the mafia would not look for me.

— Yes, but how? No body, no death! You cannot play at being dead for four days on a raised platform for the whole world to see! Even Agatha Christie would never have come up with such a scenario.

While mulling it over, the two men thought about turning the murder plot in their favor. As in judo. With a perfect model and accomplices in the Vatican, it might be possible. Better still, the mafia might think they had succeeded. And Albino Luciano would be free. On the down side, reforms wouldn't be set up, unless the new pope was a more courageous liberal pope than him.

— Imagine the puzzlement of the *mafiosi*, laughed Vittorio, if you die officially poisoned when they haven't yet put poison in your drink!

— I love your black humor Vittorio, laughed Luciani. If we found out the criminals' chosen day, we could make it all match up. We need to get ready as soon as possible, it could happen at any time.

— In the meantime, throw your chamomile down the loo! I have another idea, continued Vittorio. To do this, we need people and money. Father Dubois, the old favorite of Paul VI, has become a friend. We play squash together. He has many hidden resources. He could be useful. But he is both busy and greedy. Without money, he won't do a thing.

— You know I don't have any, Vittorio.

Vittorio suggested he used his position at the IOR. He could divert part of the mafia's piggy bank.

He knew where their stashes were hidden. In the accounts' offshore companies. He could divert huge sums, hundreds of millions of dollars and leave no trace. It would be invisible. But Luciano couldn't agree. The seventh commandment forbade it, though stealing from a thief and assassin was not clearly dealt with in the bible. Above all, he reminded Vittorio of what had happened in Switzerland. How, after having fooled crooks, he had been beaten to death.

— The road accident was an explanation for others. Have you not learned anything? You nearly lost your health, your life even, and you want to start something even more dangerous?

— You're right. But this time, I will not be able to be found.

— And what if you're wrong again? The first time you thought you were able to run between the bullets. I have thought of another way without exposing you. Call Aldo Bonassoli, our cousin. He may know how to create a good model. And if he can, I will tell Sister Vincenza, my friend Dr. Renato Buzzonetti and Cardinal Villot. And we go with it!

— But it's impossible, we can't create a false body like that, exclaimed Vittorio!

The pope liked Mark Twain. He replied with one of his lines.

— Go find out. *They didn't know it was impossible, so they did it.* Let's try, we'll see.

Monday 11 - the Vatican

On Monday 11 September, Vittorio called his cousin Aldo Bonassoli. He was in luck. Bonassoli had just returned from an exhausting oil prospecting trip in Gabon and Morocco. He was taking a break at home in Lurano, near Bergamo. They decided to meet up the following day in Milan. Vittorio would travel by plane.

After this call, Vittorio was again tempted by an embezzlement. The sums were large and the risk, small. He had the accounts, the offshore firms, numbered accounts in Switzerland, anonymous accounts in Austria. He knew how to send them. He could erase all traces of the telexes and make suspicion fall on others, such as Calvi, Sindona or Marcinkus. He could make the underworld believe the kitty was still intact when they would have lost one sixteenth of their funds. False statements were not made for nothing. They would be set up by creative accountants on his payroll, without them ever knowing who their employer was. In two years at the Institute of Works of Religion, Vittorio Petri had gone way beyond his gurus of hustle.

He remained tempted. What would his uncle say? But in fact, Albino didn't need to know. Just another lie. And it would be for him, to save him. But was it really to save his uncle or, without owning up to it, to make himself richer?

Then he thought he could always set this up a little later. Above all he was scared. "And if I had forgotten that grain of sand? Albino is right. The mafia would end up putting two and two together and finding me. I would be tortured to death. Brrr!" It was just like chess moves; you could always move one pawn but not take it back. He decided to keep that key pawn on its starting square.

Without moving it. He also remembered this aphorism by the French politician Henri Queuille, *there is no problem that an absence of a solution does not resolve.*

He put it off till later. Or to the Greek kalends.

Tuesday 12 - Milan

Aldo Bonassoli collected Vittorio Petri from Milan-Linate airport. They had a delighted hug. Aldo had no children. Vittorio was like a son to him. Aldo questioned him:

— Your call was very mysterious, what brings you here?

— I'll tell you in a moment. Let's take a walk in the Ticino neighborhood. I haven't been back for a long time; its charming with the canals.

Walks, that meant plans of illegal deeds; Bonassoli could see what was coming but as always an optimist, he said:

— Va bene let's go!

And started up his micro-Fiat 500, driving like a madman through dense traffic.

— You can get through anything with this, it's great in town!

They had to walk along the canals three times, for Aldo to take in this absurd idea. On two occasions he put his hand on his cousin's forehead in a theatrical manner. Then he remembered what they were in the process of achieving in France, himself and his associates. Which was just as absurd and impossible!

— A pity I can't check with Albino that you don't have a screw loose!

— Of course, you can check! Here, there is his direct line. It is protected. You can speak freely. If it rings for more than five times, call back later. No-one else answers this line.

— If Albino agrees that I'm not fit for the asylum, could you do something for him?

— Si, bene! I should be able to make a life-like model. I have done it for a carnival. The Duce, for instance. But it was too dangerous. I had destroyed the model. With a latex print and a system, I had invented to validate and refine the physical mold. We film different angles, and my machine creates a 3D image on the screen. It's revolutionary, shouted Aldo, as he did whenever he mentioned one of his inventions! It's not totally perfect, so I prefer to mark the model physically. But if I have to do Luciano's whole body, that will be too difficult!

— No, his false body will be shown fully dressed. And those who go very close to him will be in the know. The head and hands must be perfect. The rest can be a little imprecise.

— I love this challenge, I'll take it on! I'm bored in France, portending to look for crude oil year after year, it's tedious. But to save my dear cousin! And the Pope, to boot! Under the mafia's nose! It's exhilarating!

He hugged Vittorio.

— Grazie for bringing me this gift! Ah, there's a phone booth, it's naptime, I'll find him.

He went in and got hold of the holy father straightaway. Ten minutes later he came out aghast.

— You didn't even tell me the whole story, Vittorio. This story is quite mad. Let's settle down here, I need a triple Punt e Mes!

Once settled, Also Bonassoli and Vittorio Petri refined the battle plan of their impossible mission. Aldo would create the physical marks and video of the pope within the next three days. He hoped to be successful with his ultramodern Xerox Alto minicomputer, its graphic interface, its large memory and the special program he had made to interpret the images of the face and hands. If he had to, he would ask Vittorio to help him.

— We'll need papers for Albino, thought Vittorio out loud. He will not be able to continue using the identity of a dead man. Passport, identity card, driving license.

— I have a trustworthy system.

— It would be best for me too. To hire a car that could not be traced afterwards, the evening Albino disappears.

— I have a camera in the car. I'll take a passport compatible picture for you. For Albino, I'll do it after I have created his body marks.

Wednesday 13 - Lurano

Everything happened quickly after that. Bonassoli called an old accomplice in Paris, Jean Violet, a spook who, among other things, created credible and durable false identities. He would help out Bonassoli without any questions. Aldo would return to Rome with the papers.

Rome

That day, after two weeks of fighting with the papal administration, Alessa Lombardi was finally able to put in her agenda, Tuesday, October 10, at 10:00 a.m.:

« Pope, private audience and interview. »

She would have a good month to be prepared. The *Corriere della Sera* was interested.

Friday 15 - the Vatican

Bonassoli made an official visit to his cousin Luciani in the pontifical apartments. Two secretary priests attended part of the pope's photo shoot and the demonstration of a sin and infidelity detector.

— Have you heard of the lie detector, asked Bonassoli?

— Well, yes, we have heard about it, said one of the priests.

— Well, it works long the same principle, a detector of brainwaves, explained Bonassoli with a wicked smile.

Both secretaries stepped back. The pope was laughing under his breath. Then Luciani and his cousin retired to the private apartments for a chat. Bonassoli was carrying a lot of material which puzzled the priests. He asked for their help to carry it all, stating that he never moved around without his precious inventions.

— Completely mad, that guy, said one of the priests, when he was sure he was out of earshot.

— Mind the brainwaves, answered the other one.

When the pope and Bonassoli were alone, the latter asked Luciani to lie down on a couch in the middle of the room. He had to join his hands on his tummy, keep still and close his eyes. Then he moved a camera around him. Finally, he covered him in a thick paste. Two straws in his nostrils enabled him to breathe.

— Keep still. It's important. I'm timing you. Ten minutes. As if you were at the dentist.

Then with great care, he peeled off his skin the half-set paste.

— In a quarter of an hour, it will be dry. We will do the hands again under another angle and also your head. Lie on your front, there, just like that, lean your forehead against this cushion; your large nose needs space, fine, don't move, I'm spreading the paste.

After their long private meeting, Bonassoli left the palace with all his stuff. He needed two members of staff to help. The two secretary priests had gone.

Saturday 16 - the Vatican

The next day, the pope invited two people. He saw them separately in his private office. He explained the situation. If he remained at the helm of the Church, his life was hanging by a thread. Stepping down was no solution. He didn't want to sacrifice himself as Jesus and the early Christians had done. He wasn't that brave.

Sister Vincenza, the first of the people he spoke to, had so much love, so much respect for Albino Luciani, was so devoted to him that she accepted all his instructions. And agreed to keep silent forever.

Dr. Renato Buzzonetti was an old friend. He held the official position that would make him called to his bedside. Albino Luciani had to work hard. It was difficult for Dr. Buzzonetti to agree to produce a false death certificate when the day came. It was against professional ethics. But the equation was simple, argued Luciani.

— To save the life of a friend and a pope is worth a fake piece of paper, no?

Dr. Buzzonetti was at the end of his career, at the height of his reputation. He wasn't risking much. If he were caught out, he would say he had been negligent, tricked by low light or had a hangover. Or better still, the truth, to save the Holy Father from assassination. It was morally right. He agreed. He would get a colleague who would not even see the corpse to sign the second certificate.

— What will you do afterwards?

— I'd like to tell you my plans but it's best if I don't. For your safety and your family's, don't tell anyone.

The third person to include in the secret was the Secretary of State Jean-Marie Villot. Without his support, the trick could not work. He was essential to its success. Jean-Paul I decided to put off this crucial meeting till the day after next. He didn't want to call him out again on a Sunday. The cardinal hated it. So he asked him for dinner on the Monday evening. They could talk before the meal.

Sunday 17 - the Vatican

At 12 noon, the pope said the Angelus from his window for the faithful on St. Peter's square.

Monday 18 - the Vatican

On Monday evening, the pope received his State Secretary, Cardinal Jean-Marie Villot in his official office.

— Thank you for coming, Your Eminence. Two weeks ago, I warned you of the attack that was being prepared against me on Wednesday 6. Thank you again for your actions to cover up my escape.

— Holy Father, may I ask you a question that has been bothering me for the last two weeks?

— Go ahead.

— Nothing happened on 6. Were you really in danger? Were you correctly informed?

— I have an ugly answer. Are you ready to hear me out?

— Yes.

Luciani told him what had happened at Cortina d'Ampezzo, and that he would be poisoned shortly.

Villot was shocked. Under his cold administrator's appearances, he had feelings.

— I cannot continue with this threat, said John Paul I and I don't want dirty money to be laundered again.

Cardinal Villot said nothing. He knew quite a bit about the goings-on at the IOR, with the approval of the former pope. He was not proud of it.

Luciani then spoke of his zugzwang that whatever he did or didn't do, he would lose. Then he concluded with his decision: on the day of his poisoning, he would leave his post discreetly. To step down would resolve nothing. He would play dead, to pull the rug from under the mafia's feet. He acknowledged he was beaten. Perhaps the next pope would manage things better than himself.

— Will you help me to do this? Without you, nothing can happen. I'm asking you, not as your boss, but as a humble sinner asks of a Christian. It would be your last task for me. Then I will disappear forever. I will only be a man among men.

Cardinal Villot was old, he was 74 and knew he was very ill. According to his doctor, he had only 6 months to live; he thought for a long while, then asked to withdraw to a corner of the room to pray. After his prayer, his mind was made up. If he helped to save a pure heart, he could stand before his God. Otherwise, his passive complicity with the actions of the Bank of the Vatican would weigh heavily at the moment of the last Judgment. He agreed without reserve. He was even freed from a great weight of guilt. He had obeyed his superior, pope Paul VI, because he had vowed him obedience. But he wasn't at ease with himself. This new idealistic pope, with a youth's temperament, was giving him the opportunity to redeem himself. He felt light and happy. During the meal, both men, who had, in the previous three weeks, not trusted each other, were now serene and even jolly at times.

THE DEADLOCK

19 - 27 September 1978

Tuesday 19 - USA

Paul Burbon, director of the powerful NSA was sitting at his desk, in Maryland near Washington.

— Who is this?

— Never mind, just listen. Your daughter Nelly is with us. . .

— Nooooo!

— Be quiet, stay in control or you will not see her alive again. If you do as we say, we will free her unharmed.

Paul automatically switched on the tracking procedure.

— How do I know you are telling the truth?

— Call your wife. I'll call you in 15 minutes.

The caller hung up. The detection program showed nothing.

Paul called his wife.

— Did Nelly come back with the nanny?

— In fact, no, and it's bothering me. Why are you asking? Your voice sounds odd.

— Just something that's bothering me. Could you call me when Nelly is home?

His wife's voice rose.

— What are you not telling me, for goodness' sake? Tell me, what is up with Nelly?

— Are you sitting down?

— No

— Sit down.

— No, I'm listening, go ahead!

— I had a call a few minutes ago. She may have been abducted.

He heard a dull sound. His wife should have sat down. He called his neighbor and asked her to drop in next door. She had the key. His wife had felt faint.

The phone rang. It was the kidnapper.

— Here is Nelly.

— Daddy, the man says he's not nasty, but I'd rather be with you. When will you come and get me?

— Very soon darling, be good. I'm sending you a kiss.

— It's no longer darling, said a male voice. These are our conditions: the US stop helping the pope. Leave him be. If you don't, you will never see your kid again. In any case, not alive. If you obey, she will be returned to you at the end of the month.

— You know who I am.

— Yes, of course.

— In my job, I have the means to find you.

— We are aware of that. We know how powerful you are. Your daughter will come back to you, fit and well as soon as it's over. We don't want you to resent us. It would not serve our interests. Do as we say, and it will end well. You can call the police if you like, we are not bothered.

He hung up. The tracing system had failed. The call had been recorded but was encrypted and he was the only one who could listen to it. The bastards were well informed. In the very heart of the NSA. Only the mafia had such power and wanted the pope out.

Paul went home. His wife and his other children needed him.

The nanny was overwhelmed. The child had suddenly disappeared while she was playing in the park. They told her to go home and didn't tell her off. The older ones hadn't yet gotten home from school. Nelly would be spending time at her aunt for some ten days or so. Her brother and sister were not to worry about her, they were children. If Nelly was returned, there would be time yet to tell them what'd happened. Otherwise, best not to think about it. Paul put the conditions to his wife. It was top secret, but he didn't care. After the older ones had gotten home, they had to look normal. When the children were in bed, they discussed the situation all night long, without finding an answer.

Wednesday 20 - Rome

At the same time, in Rome, Nancy Jones' NSA team was listening in on a conversation between a Sicilian godfather and Cighi. John Paul's assassination would take place on the evening of September 28. A teaspoonful of digitalis would be added to his evening chamomile. Death would look just like a heart attack, as long as there was no autopsy. Cighi had dirt on Cardinal Villot, like he did on so many others in Italy. It was his forte. On the night of 28–29, he would tell Villot he had no personal interest in having an autopsy carried out and that a quick embalming would be perfectly suitable.

Such callousness was horrid, but Nancy could easily set aside her feelings, so as not to be overwhelmed. Like a nurse in intensive care. Otherwise, she would lose all her efficiency. Her job was to get to know of filth and follow it up. She wired a coded telex to Paul Burbon, the director of the NSA. With the time difference, he got to read it as he arrived at his office on the morning of Wednesday, September 20.

Wednesday 20 - USA

After a sleepless night debating with his wife about what they should or should not do, he left for his office. He would have more leverage there than if he stayed at home. No-one knew, no-one must know where the Director of the NSA and his family lived. It was top secret. They lived under a false identity in a smart neighborhood in Washington. It was normal practice for high-ranking secret agents. He got transported by car, sheltered from rockets, he had a discreet guard. His family, his house, his neighborhood were all protected. It was clearly a paper wall for the mafia. As was his own implication in the pope's rescue. The Mob had got hold of secret defense information. A mole at the White House? In the West wing? Plausible. He was thinking this through while being driven towards Maryland.

"It's not difficult to spot us, it's dead easy in fact. Trips can be put together easily with regular observation over several weeks. Even if they change all the time."

He was almost relieved by this old-fashioned hypothesis. He still had to resolve the matter of his role. What could he do to save Nelly? Inform the police? She would die long before she would be found.

Paul Burbon arrived at Fort Meade, headquarters of the NSA, at 9 a.m. With his coffee, he read the text Nancy

Jones had sent from Rome at 2 p.m. He leant back in his rocking chair, asked not to be disturbed and fell asleep while thinking.

He spent all day like this, not telling anyone, in spite of the huge power of his organization. His wife had made him promise he wouldn't try anything that could put Nelly's life in danger. He had agreed. He knew of the collateral damage one was exposed to once the enormous machine was set going. For now, they had decided to wait. To see if a subtle way through turned up. He spent the day waiting for it to come up on the day's routine. There was no breakthrough. It was a black hole. Beaten. Weakened. Emptied from within.

Thursday 21 - USA

Next morning, Burbon felt better. He and his wife had slept despite everything. It was difficult to keep their sadness and their worry from their other children; to appear cheerful. They did their best. But the kids felt something was up. During the night, they had again tried to work around possibilities to rescue their youngest one, but nothing concrete had come up.

After breakfast, the matter of the kids' safety came up while they were on their way to school. They considered moving that day to one of the NSA's safe houses. But it would be no good. The Mob had such a lever with Nelly. It wouldn't need another which would have the opposite effect. On the other hand, they needed to be ready to move afterwards. For good. Their cover had been blown. What a life his family had! Their social network would have to be started all over again. For the first time in this life, Paul thought about changing jobs. Spying wasn't an occupation for a family man.

At the office, Paul Burbon realized he hadn't informed the President of anything the day before. Nancy's message was still in abeyance. He read it again. The pope's poisoning was scheduled for the evening, in Rome time, on Thursday, September 28. It was obvious. He had to tell the President. What was wrong this time?

If the pope survived, his daughter would die. The kidnappers had been clear.

Nelly would be saved if he killed the pope. Nelly or the pope. The pope or Nelly. It was obvious. But what about his duty as an officer? His honor versus the life of a four-year-old. That was obvious, too.

Friday 22 - Washington

Paul Burbon deliberately gave the President a false date. The 29 instead of the 28. If John Paul I didn't protect himself before 29, he would die on the 28 and Nelly would be freed.

He was wrong, of course, because as soon as the pope had learned that he would have poison in this chamomile, he would throw it down the loo, whatever the date. Burbon had ruined his reputation for nothing. The pope wouldn't drink his chamomile and his little girl would be killed. Thankfully for him, he was not aware of this when he left the Oval Office.

After the director of the NSA had left, President Carter called the pope. He gave him the news, with regret and compassion. A murder by digitalis was confirmed on Friday, September 29. Neither sooner nor later. The conspirators wanted all the details sorted out for a set date. The pope thanked him for his precious and disinterested support.

Friday 22 - the Vatican

After the call, Luciani had second thoughts. Was his duty not to stay at the helm? Does a captain leave a ship when it's sinking? For the Church was truly sinking morally. He hovered between his will to live and his commitment as a shepherd.

If he stayed, he would die without changing anything. His death would be pointless. It would be spectacular but serve no purpose. "And if I changed one thing before disappearing? It's all so confused. Yet I know who the most corrupt ones are, Marcinkus, Mannini and de Strobel. I'm going to oust them, and place my successor before they can even blink an eye."

He prepared the paperwork to sack three people and nominate another three with the help of his Secretary of State. After that, his sense of guilt lessened. It was too late for birth control. The upturning of the papal encyclical, Humanae Vitae by Paul VI would not happen in a jiffy.

Friday 22- Rome

— It's ready. It's just like him. Beyond my wildest hopes! It's a perfect illusion. You can come and collect it when you like, said an excited Aldo Bonassoli on the phone!

— Wow! I'm leaving today. Can you put me up, Vittorio Petri answered?

— We'll set up an inflatable mattress under the proton console, do come!

— See you tonight.

Saturday 23 - Lurano

Vittorio was spending time with his cousin Aldo Bonassoli in the village of Lurano, between Bergamo and Milan. The journey from Rome had seemed long and he enjoyed a restful night. The evening before, they had admired the model of the pope lifeless; then dined on excellent dishes they had prepared together.

They wrapped the fake body with care. The material had been extraordinarily successful, elastic and already simulating body stiffness after embalming.

— It's extraordinary, the texture of semi-flexible skin, it really looks like Albino, a work of art, exclaimed Vittorio!

— Thank you. The mixture worked, in one week exactly. It's a better likeness than Tussaud's and Grévin

Museums where it takes twenty people and six months. I worked day and night and I'm exhausted, but proud!

— Pity it has to end up inside four coffins in a funeral crypt. No-one will know . . . if it goes all well.

— Anonymous glory, the best! But you and Albino will know, it's enough to satisfy my enormous ego!

Aldo explained to Vittorio how to fit different parts of the body. How to match parts like the head and the hands closely and invisibly.

— Albino will be alone when he does it. And it's heavy, it's his weight. You will show him well in advance, so he can practice like you now. He must put it together on the bed. To avoid having to carry the whole body.

Then they put Albino Luciani's facsimile in separate parts into two big bags.

— It's heavy, as you say, said Vittorio, carrying one of the bags over his shoulders.

— The composite material and the latex weigh next to nothing. But it is the ballast. The weight must be the same as Albino's. Thank God, he's light. Arrivederci Vittorio, don't drive as fast as I do, I don't have another model! Ah, and should we agree a code? A silly phrase he would say on the phone, like the free French did on the radio during the war?

— *Why are you coughing*, for instance?

— That reminds me of something, he smiled. Yes, *why are you coughing?* He would just say that and hang up. That's all. We would know he is alive and he's still able to dial a friend. And say a "break a leg" from me.

Sunday September 24

When Albino Luciani appeared at his window for his last Angelus, he put his heart into it. There were many pilgrims on St. Peter's Square. A sign of a friendly farewell, he thought with emotion.

Tuesday 26 - the Vatican

At 9 at night, Vittorio, loaded as a donkey and trying not to be seen, slipped into the gardens of Chateau Saint-Ange. He operated the secret passages and found himself on the aerial medieval path above the city. Then, he did a second trip for the other bag. Sitting on the floor, he waited in the half-light behind the papal library.

At 9:30, the panel slid open and the pope appeared. Vittorio told his uncle what Aldo had shown him. They tried putting together and dismantling the replica, first both of them, then Albino on his own. He was flabbergasted by the quality of the look-alike.

They agreed on the code: *Why are you coughing?*

— Don't forget to flush your chamomile down the loo, tomorrow evening, advised Vittorio!

— What do you think I have been doing for a week, smiled Albino? I couldn't forgo Sister Vicenza's morning coffee, I took the risk. While imploring the Lord.

They hid the bags behind the library, then Vittorio disappeared the same way.

Wednesday 27 - the Vatican

At his last general audience, the pope refused again to be carried by other men on the *Sedia gestatoria* seat. Every week, it was presented to him with great compunction and obstinacy by the Curia's fundamentalists. As he stepped in, he grinned. The crowd cheered him. His entire charisma was required to heat a room with such hideous architecture. He spoke of charity, read out a poem by Trilussa in romanesco, the Roman dialect, and chatted with a child. He felt good. He was going to be free.

Wednesday 27 - Rome

— *Is everything ready?*
— *Yes, for tomorrow night.*
— *Tonight would be better.*
— *Impossible. There is a shift rotation there.*
— *OK*

It was the transcript of a phone conversation Nancy Jones' team had just caught. Something intrigued her. She re-read it.

— *Is everything ready?*
— *Yes, for tomorrow night.*

Tomorrow is the 28th. But the president told the pope on the 29th! NASA was also listening to the line. Unofficially. She checked. The President or Burbon got the day wrong.

The attack would take place a night earlier. Did it matter? The pope had to watch everything he drank. Whatever the day. On the other hand, the message had been so clear, the date, the time, the digitalis, the evening chamomile. Perhaps the pope would drink it with no concern whilst it wasn't yet the 29th. She wasn't willing to take that risk. She checked the whereabouts of Carter. In the USSR with Brejnev. She called Paul, at NASA headquarters. He would ask the vice-president to call the pope. Paul Burbon could not be contacted till the following evening, East coast time. In any case, with the time difference, it was too tight.

Then, Nancy Jones did what she should have never done: she warned Vittorio. The attack would be next evening, not the following evening. She told him the truth. Who she worked for. Carter had known about this through her. She made him swear not to say anything. For his part, he told her about the trick to swap bodies and the plan for the pope to escape. They were quits.

Vittorio took a detour via the official entrance flanked by Swiss Guards to warn his uncle: the attack attempt and his escape were set for the next evening. Albino was surprised his nephew was so well informed.

— Don't ask, Uncle, I can't tell you. Believe my word. I am 100% sure. It's for tomorrow. Tomorrow evening, I will wait for you as arranged.

They hugged as though it would be the last time and Vittorio set off to find Nancy. They hugged too, at length and tenderly, teasing each other about their secrets. Then they went to dinner in Trastevere. The evening was so mild! After August's heatwave, the temperature in September was perfect. How far they were from shady financiers, corrupt prelates, crooks, spies and poisoners! The noise of dishing up, multiple conversations, shouts of joy provided lovely sounds on the dimmed terrace. At another table, sat their journalist friend, Alessa Lombardi, with her current boyfriend. They took their grappas and coffee together. They only talked about inconsequential things, as though the troubles they were going through had been left at the entrance, in a virtual hallway.

At the Vatican, the pope was giving final instructions to sister Vincenza, Cardinal Villot and Dr. Buzzonetti: it was going to be tomorrow evening. He signed the dismissal paperwork, with immediate effect, of Paul Marcinkus, Luigi Mannini and Peregrino de Strobel. The documents were dated the same day and were legally binding. He added the nomination decrees of three replacements, then deposited all six documents in the drawer which only the secretary of state had access to. He had a key. The pope told him where to find these papers, which would come into force on September 29.

After withdrawing, he prepared his ceremonial vestments which were going to clothe the deceased body. It had been agreed that only sister Vincenza, Cardinal Villot and Dr. Buzzonetti would dress the mannequin which would be discovered at dawn on the 29th, in bed and in his pajamas; as Albino Luciano would have settled it on the evening of the 28th. Sister Vincenza would stay awake the whole night of 28 to 29th in an armchair outside the pope's bedroom door. She would allow no-one in. Apart from Cardinal Villot and Dr. Buzzonetti, in the morning.

But meanwhile, informers of Elio Cighi were telling him what was plotted in the pope's palace. He joined bits of information: the pope could well be preparing to escape. Once again as he had done on September 5. Thinking back, Cighi was sure John Paul had had a "diplomatic illness" from September 5 to 8. A cold had been too convenient.

An old cardinal from the Curia had spoken to him about old ancestral passages, too. It was logical, the kings of Naples had had some built in the 18th century, to get away by sea. Only Louis XIV hadn't built any at Versailles and Louis XVI had been plucked like a novice. The priest had heard vague rumors of two possible ways out. The first could be around Viale Vaticano 50, west of the Vatican, beyond the old town walls. The other possible exit was at Castel Sant'Angelo, to the east. The informer knew nothing more. He had no idea where these passages, if they existed, started from inside the Vatican. That was still something.

Elio Cighi dialed a number in Palermo.

The Switch

September 28, 1978

Thursday 28 – the Vatican

The following day went by. The pope had, for once, followed the routine dictated by his secretariat. Audiences, a meeting with Costa Rica's ambassador, a siesta, a meeting with a few Church high dignitaries to deal with nominations, beatification projects, a pilgrimage and taking part in an inauguration.

He ate dinner on his own and asked not to be disturbed before the next morning, when he withdrew to his private apartment.

He swung the panel in the library, then dragged both bags, one after the other, along the floor to his bedroom and started to assemble his double.

— Hi you, we won't have known each other very long. If it works, you're going to have a global destiny. Good luck. And please don't wake up like Pinocchio did. Promise? Don't trick me.

The dummy agreed, put on its pajamas and got into bed.

The pope put his ring down, on the bedside table. But he kept his glasses on.

He said out loud with a malicious grin like Captain Haddock, one of his favorite characters,

— At least the Vaticanologists will have a mystery to solve.

Once in the bathroom, he dyed his hair black, the color it was when he was young, leaving gray at the temples. He shoved the dyeing stuff into the bag, including the waste, and put in his new soft contact lenses. He had tried them out in Cortina. He was unrecognizable with his baseball cap. At most, someone might say, "ah! I've seen that chap before".

Then he dressed like a tourist, with a multi-pocket waistcoat, jeans, jacket, his camera. His backpack, a gift from Vittorio, half mountain bag, half travel bag, was made of thin and strong fabric. He filled it with what he had planned, that is, very little. He carried the dollars and travelers checks on him. At the last moment, he left his watch, with a twinge, on the bedside table. It bore an inscription by his mother on the back. If the watch were to disappear as well as the glasses, it would really be a bit much.

Then it took him a long time to check the place. To be sure he'd not left anything behind. His ordinary shoes were, as they should be, in the bedroom and not on his feet. His socks, underwear, shirt and trousers were also there. It was easier for the cassock: he wasn't going to leave with it. He went through all the rooms with a vague feeling something wasn't quite right. No, he couldn't find anything, it all seemed in order. The time had come to say goodbye to this strange place where he had spent the most intense month of his whole life. And yet he couldn't leave it. He sat for a while to allow his mind to join his body. A month earlier, he had experienced the rarest change of status a man could go through. And he was preparing now for an even crazier leap into the unknown. He no longer felt light and free as he had done the previous evening. He felt stressed. He began to pray, which helped him when he had doubts or worries. He prayed for a long time. Too long. Vittorio was waiting for him. He went back to his sleeping dummy to check his watch. Half past nine already! He was late. "I know what was wrong! What was bothering me! The bags in which my dummy was delivered, I have to take them back. Where are they? He found them half hidden under the bed, in the bedroom. "Mustn't leave them here. Nor behind the bookcase. I'll give them to Vittorio who will use them for something else."

He finally left through the now familiar passage. The light was falling outside. It was still hot. He felt a light breeze on his face as he walked towards Saint-Angelo Castle. The winds of freedom, he thought, happily,

— Phew, I'm no longer pope! He whispered to himself, laughing.

Thursday 28 – Rome

As agreed, Vittorio was waiting for his uncle, in a car rental under a false name. He was parked right near the Saint-Angelo Castle.

He outlined the main steps of their plan.

He would take Albino to the station. He, Vittorio, would stay in Rome at IOR as if nothing had happened. He would take the car back to the rental agency on the 30th. On the 29th, he would take a day off. Officially, to recover from the distress. In fact, to go into hiding, until the pope was placed in his tomb. If the trick were to be uncovered, it would be better if he couldn't be found. He would only be safe when the pseudo-pope was buried in the four coffins of the necropolis. Before that, there would be a few difficult days of public exposure.

Albino Luciani would go to Bari on the train. Then take a one-way ferry ticket to Greece. Patras and so forth. An average retired European cultural tourist. He would come back in a couple of years, via Yugoslavia and settle in the Ticino. In a modest flat already bought for him by Aldo Bonassoli. He would teach Greek and Latin in a private school. Or be just a retired bricklayer. He would get a monthly pay on an account opened under his new name at UBS in Lugano. Albino had found it difficult to accept charity. Wasn't charity encouraged by the Church, Aldo had retorted? He would get no pension for having been priest, bishop or pope; although he had worked his whole life. It was right he got a pension. Albino was still resisting. Wouldn't Aldo suffer financially with that unexpected expense? Aldo Bonassoli reassured him: he had earned, in France, more money than he could ever spend during a century with his invention of oil detectors. Albino accepted.

At this moment of his daydream, Albino opened the passenger door. Vittorio turned his head just in time to see him collapse next to him. His cap had fallen on the gear lever. In the next moment, Vittorio himself was pulled from his seat and knocked out.

Both killers had been standing guard around Saint-Angelo Castle for twenty-four hours. They didn't know where, when or how their target would show up. If it showed up. They had spotted the car in which Vittorio was waiting. It could be linked with the target. When he had sprung from nowhere running towards the car, they rushed and knocked him down just to make sure. They would check later if it was the target. And it was the right one. They had been lucky. They threw each of the muzzled and handcuffed prisoners in a car boot. Theirs and Vittorio's. They then set off. Everything had happened very quickly and discreetly. Vittorio had parked in a deserted part of Piazza Adriana.

At the same time, the second commando was keeping watch on the other side of the Vatican, in Viale Vaticano. Their victim, a man aged 65 could appear within one hundred meters from the pink Venetian house with a garden at 50 Viale Vaticano. They had been on the lookout since the previous day.

Vittorio tried to move as soon as he woke up. His hands were tied together behind his back. It seemed rather cowardly. "Handcuffs", he thought. Suddenly, he felt a violent headache. He felt like vomiting, screaming. But his mouth was shut, stuck. He tried to open it. Impossible. "If I puke, I'm screwed", while concentrating hard to control his body. He was lying on his left side. The floor was hard. He felt his bones hurt on the bumps. That was it, he was in a car boot. He wasn't blindfolded, but this meant nothing as it was pitch black. He forgot about his physical pains and began to feel fearful. This was the end of the road. He hoped it would be quick and painless.

Albino had lost consciousness on opening the car door. He was waking to life in an oven and hurt all over. He tried to think about Vittorio. Hoping he wouldn't be in the same position. But there was little hope. Where had their plan gone wrong? He tried to think; he gave up because of his throbbing headache. "Never mind now, what's coming is clear. And gloomy at the same time. Better to die now rather than to suffer for weeks the fate of Aldo Moro and die in the end. He tried to pray, but this no longer worked."

He tried to assess the journey. Its length, the noise in the streets. The stops at red lights. How long had he been unconscious? After ten, twenty, thirty minutes - impossible to estimate - the car slowed down, he felt painful bumps and then the car stopped. The engine stopped. Darkness and silence.

The boot opened. He noticed the glow of the soft September night behind two chaps who pulled him out roughly, got him to stand and tethered his ankles. He almost asked for his baseball cap to annoy them and show he wasn't afraid. But he refrained. What would be the point of humor in those circumstances? He, as a Christian, had to prepare to meet his God. These two men didn't count any more.

Vittorio appeared at his side in the same situation. They looked at each other, but couldn't speak. They were ordered to move forward. They were reassured to keep them docile, the same way the SS did. Further to the right, they would be tethered and held in a small shed while waiting for the ransom.

But the killers hadn't even bothered to hide their faces. Which left the victims in no doubt as to what was awaiting them.

Although one never knows; they were proudly and mechanically stepping towards certain death.

They were progressing. The ground was dry and hard, with stones and a bit of dry grass. They could only progress slowly, because of their chains. They couldn't attempt anything. They carried on, following their executioners' orders. Ten meters, thirty meters, fifty? It wasn't a house that appeared, but an old bathtub. The sort one uses to water the cows. They were probably in a field outside of Rome, abandoned for years. The ideal spot to get rid of them. Right next to the bathtub, they noticed with horror white polyethylene cans. Acid. To eliminate their bodies. At this point, they were hoping to be killed before being showered with acid. But the mafia was sadistic.

Just then, Vittorio's sphincters gave up. He let go. He swore against his body betraying him and keeping him from dying with dignity.

Albino looked at him. It was a smile, "Farewell, I love you". Vittorio glanced at him with love. Then Albino turned his head and stared in front of him. He could no longer see the bathtub or the cans. His eyes were looking into the distance, on the horizon of the buzz of the city. He was humming a psalm of victory, love, hope and eternal life.

Whereas Vittorio was hypnotized by the bathtub and the cans. In any case, it wasn't milk. He tried to calm down, to breathe deeply while waiting for the bullet in his head.

Pop! Pop!

"Oh, what sadists! They are opening the champagne before bumping us off!" thought Vittorio, outraged and conscious that this was one of his last thoughts.

They heard footsteps behind them.

"They are going to shoot us in the head, champagne flutes in hand!"

Vittorio was no longer afraid. Albino was already somewhere else.

— Your kidnappers are dead. Don't be afraid, said a male voice. Don't move. I'm going to release your arms, your ankles and your mouth. Keep still, don't run off. I'm your friend said the man unchaining them.

Once freed, Albino knelt down and thanked the Lord.

Vittorio walked awkwardly to the car, took a sports bag from the back seat and went to get changed a bit further away.

The man asked Albino to go back to their car and wait for him. Then he picked up both bodies, lifted them up and into the bathtub, opened the containers and poured the contents on the bodies. He moved away quickly. Toxic fumes rose in the dusk.

The man came back after a long while.

Albino Luciani thanked him for saving their lives.

He asked formally:

— To whom do I have the honor?

— Abbot Dubois. Yves Dubois. And you?

— Retired bricklayer. I've also been pope.

— Pleased to meet you, Your Holiness.

— I am not anymore. But ho . . ., how did you save us at the last minute?

— Oh, said Father Dubois, today I'm only a hitman. Giving a hand to my American colleague. She's behind the wheel, in the car over there. We help each other out from time to time. Goodbye, happy to have met you.

He left with the killers' car, followed by the other car. Vittorio identified an elusive silhouette evoking Nancy.

Father Dubois, by pure provocation, left the car fifty meters from a quilt and blanket factory; Dalo's coverage in Rome for the Palermo boss. Dubois thought joyfully: "Dalo will think it's the Roman godfather who had his two soldati killed, for territorial reasons!"

Both survivors left the wasteland in the hire car. Vittorio was shaking. His teeth were chattering. They stopped. Albino, who had already gotten over the shock of a papal election, was doing better. He gave Vittorio a bar of chocolate and a drink. He took over the driving and drove to Rome station. He asked Vittorio, with kindness:

— How are you feeling?

They were sitting in the car, with the engine off. They had plenty of time before the train's departure.

— I'm going to be OK. You're a great character! What a pity you can't remain pope, you would have done a wonderful job.

— I had a choice to make and neither was good. It was about survival. I don't regret it. Do you think you could do one more thing for me?

— Of course.

— It's upsetting that Nina, Ettore and your sister think I am dead. We couldn't tell them anything beforehand, it was too dangerous. But I think we can risk it now. When you feel better, could you go and see your mom and dad and tell them I am safe? Just those three, no one else. They mustn't let anyone know about the sham. After they saw what the killer was about the other day, they'll understand they have to keep quiet. What do you think?

— That bothered me too. They'll be sad for a few days. Nothing to be done. They'll come to Rome for your funeral. I'll tell them then.

— God willing! It'll be the same lapse of time as between Christ's crucifixion and resurrection. It is not without irony, said the ex-pope with a smile. Nina has a naive belief in God, she won't let us down. Her heart will have to keep going. You'll be gentle, won't you?

— Yes, Uncle, don't worry. Go with peace in mind; take care! Thanks for the adventure!

The station was full of life, noise, smells, rumors. The crowd was buzzing to and from the different destinations. The hubbub made them feel secure after their ordeal. They felt better. Normal life was taking over again.

Vittorio and Albino shared an emotional hug on the platform. They knew they could never see each other again. Then, Albino stepped into the night train to Bari. Without looking back.

THE TRICK

September 29—October 4, 1978

Friday 29 – the Vatican

Cardinal Villot was sleeping with one eye open, owing to what was going on, on the floor above. He lay fully dressed on his bed, ready for anything. He jumped up when he heard a noise at the door. It was one of the Curie's most conservative cardinals. It was half past two in the morning. His visitor was not pulling punches. The impact of his speech contrasted with his soft tone.

— Please excuse my nocturnal intrusion your Eminence, but the subject is of enormous importance for the Church.

— I'm listening, your Eminence.

— His Holiness seemed quite unwell to many of us last night. He complained about a discomfort in his chest. I'm very concerned about his health. I hope it's a false alarm and he will have recovered and be among us, fully fit, this morning. But I was so worried I took it upon myself to disturb you. I daren't bother his Holiness. He must rest after last evening's exhaustion.

Villot knew perfectly well this was nonsense. He had spent more time than anyone else with the pope the previous day, so he was perfectly aware of how good he was. But he just simply replied:

— I can understand your fear. May I suggest we say a prayer together for the Pope's health?

Both cardinals knelt on the floor and prayed for a while.

— Well, your Eminence, come to the point, said Villot rather abruptly as he stood up again.

— You're right. If Gianpaolo did die this night, you never know, God's hand is so unpredictable, it would be your duty as State Secretary and Camerlengo to destroy the pope's last orders. In order not to trouble our next pontificate, who could have a different approach.

— And what makes you think I could do such a thing, asked Villot, rather upset?

— I heard that some ill-intentioned people hold an incriminating file against you. I also seem to have understood that these people didn't want several things to happen. If they were to happen, nevertheless, these people might release some damaging reports about you. Being aware of these facts, here I am, as a brother and a friend to beg you to try and avoid such regrettable events.

— I'm listening Eminence, said Villot coldly.

— In case of His Holiness's premature death, it would be advisable not to have an autopsy performed. A corporal intrusion on the sacred Holy Father would be unnecessary, the Pope being ill. A prompt embalming would allow for the ritual lying in state to the public, without any delay, which would also, thankfully, shorten the interregnum.

The absence of an autopsy suited Villot. He, too, had a plan for the embalming. He was prepared to go along with the three dismissals for his own sake. He knew where the bullet would come from. He had to be extremely careful. He thought: "I tried, didn't make it, I've already saved the Pope, which should be enough for my redemption. Now I must work on my salvation on earth".

He nodded and dismissed his visitor.

At 4:45 a.m., as per the plan, Sister Vincenza discovered the Pope's corpse. As planned, she called Cardinal Villot who came immediately. And as planned, he called Doctor Buzzonetti who came to the Vatican right away. Doctor Renato Buzzonetti confirmed, as planned, the death by heart attack just before midnight. He established the death certificate.

Around 7 o'clock, while the three people in the know were dressing the dummy, the two Signoracci brothers, Ernesto and Renato, who had embalmed the three previous popes, dropped by. The Signoracci said that the

Vatican had called their Medical Institute earlier on. It must have been his night visitor. But unfortunately, they were too late, as other embalmers were already on the job. Villot paid them better than if they had done the work and made them promise absolute confidentiality on this very embarrassing matter for the Vatican. It was the result of a mixture of competence due to the emotion stirred by His Holiness's passing. If ever journalists or whoever were to ask them if they had embalmed the pope, their answer would be "not comment" or "professional secret".

After that interruption, Cardinal Villot, Sister Vincenza and Doctor Buzzonetti proceeded to dress the corpse with the traditional suit of vestments for exposure to the public. The defunct Pope wore a soft tiara, white socks, mules, a white cassock under a red one. His hands, holding a rosary, were crossed. His head rested on the stole covering a heavy velvet garnet cushion. His face was serene. The staging was perfect.

When everything was ready, the staff were invited to the papal apartments later that morning. Villot explained to them that they must not approach his Holy Father from less than three meters away. The doctor feared the presence of a very serious virus which could have caused the heart attack. Which was why, after the embalmers had finished their work, Cardinal Villot, Sister Vincenza and Doctor Buzzonetti alone had dressed His Holiness in order to protect everyone. Moreover, those five people would go into isolation. Meanwhile, to be on the safe side, it would be better not to get near the body or anyone who had touched him. Rumors of the risk of infection spread. Visitors were kept at a distance. On that same day, the body was taken to the Clementina Room and the doors were locked. The following day, the remains of John Paul I were taken to Saint Peter's Basilica, escorted by the Swiss Guard and followed by a procession of prelates holding candles and chanting prayers, in front of the world's cameras. For four days, the faithful queued at a distance to honor the smiling pope one last time. In Lurano, Bonassoli savored the universal pictures of his unknown work of art. Vittorio was doing the same thing from the apartment of one of Nancy's friends, who had lent it for a few days. He asked Nancy if he had seen her, during the night of the 28th, driving a car with Abbé Dubois. On a wasteland between Cinecitta and the racecourse. She put her hand on his forehead. And very tenderly.

— Have a rest my love, you really need it after all these big emotions.

He told her what had happened on the 28th in the evening. That they both had been saved seemed to her miraculous. She was smiling like Leonardo da Vinci's Madonna.

On September 29, a subordinate reported to Dalo. The two hideouts around the Vatican hadn't produced anything. The car of the Saint-Angelo team had been found in the morning, parked beside the blanket factory. But nothing had been found at the usual execution spots. The bathtub near Cinecitta had been used.

— The message is clear, he's behind this, fulminated the Palermo boss! It's that Roman son of a bitch, that bastard defending his territory tooth and nail. What a fool! He has another thing coming!

He couldn't have given a dam for the loss of two clumsy soldiers, as long as that shitty pope was dead, and he'd got the car back. He was over the moon and so happy that he generously told his subordinate he was forgiven.

Friday 29 – Washington

Paul Burbon was listening to the seven o'clock news whilst getting dressed. The new pope had just died from a heart attack after only 33 days as a pontiff. Paul felt intense joy. He had nothing against the man. But his death would give his child a chance to live.

— It's not an ordinary kidnapping, he told his wife. They are aware of my position and my tracing capabilities. They know that if they don't give us Nelly back, they will regret it for the rest of their lives. That's why I'm rather optimistic. If they are reasonable. And I'm under the impression that they are. Immensely cruel but reasonable.

He left home at eight o'clock. Nelly was playing on the garden lawn with her favorite teddy, between two flower beds.

In the afternoon, the President called Paul Burbon. He was sad about the pope's passing away.

— You told me he would be poisoned on the 29th, not the 28th. Your Roman team made a mistake.

Jimmy Carter had great human assets but could really split hairs on details. Burbon had got to know him in the last two years. He was expecting this phone call.

— Yes, Mr. President, it also intrigued me this morning, when I heard the sad news. I've checked since. The Roman team did the right thing. They told me the 28th. I made the mistake. I'm sorry, Mr. President. My resignation will be on your desk before this evening.

— Thank you, Paul. He who does nothing never makes mistakes. I'm refusing it. That will stop you from having to write it. Do congratulate your Roman team on my behalf! Who's at the head?

— Nancy Jones, Mr. President. And thanks for your indulgence.

— See you soon, Paul.

October 4 – Rome

The Requiem mass took place in Rome, on October 4th, with tens of thousands of believers in Saint Peter's Square. For four days, hundreds of thousands had walked past the dummy made to measure by the skillful Aldo Bonassoli.

The pseudo-corpse of Albino Luciani was laid in three coffins inside a fourth one made of marble from Carrara, in the papal crypt, to Vittorio's relief while he watched the ceremony on television. Someone else was also watching it, from somewhere in Greece.

This was only the beginning of the controversy on the odd circumstances of the death of John Paul I. A lot of ink was to flow discussing his earlier good health, the loss of his written orders, the absence of an autopsy, the quick embalming and above all, the disappearance of his glasses. The Vatican always stuck to the official version: natural death.

Corriere della Sera

Ante cum clave 1
> *The brief pontificate of John Paul I ended today with his solemn funeral. In ten days, the doors of the Sistine Chapel will*

*close again on the 111 cardinal electors, to elect his successor by
a qualified two-thirds majority. Everyone will still have in
mind the sudden, unexpected death of the "smiling pope". Since
his death on the night of September 28-29, rumors have been
flying. Why didn't he report feeling ill when he phoned his
doctor on the evening of the 28th? Why did the state documents
he was working on evaporate? Why was there no autopsy?
Why are the appointed embalmers as silent as carp? Why did
the Holy Father's glasses disappear? Many unanswered
questions. There is one official answer: a heart attack. As
attested by the death certificate signed by two eminent
practitioners.
Alessa Lombardi, Corriere della Sera
Tomorrow: the issues of the conclave.*

THE LION

October 1978—January 1979

October 16 – the Vatican

Another conclave was set up ten days later, on October 14th. On October 16th, after eight rounds of elections, the Polish Cardinal Karol Wojtyla was elected pope, taking the name of John Paul II.

January 1979 – the Vatican

Jimmy Carter paid a visit to John Paul II in January. He invited him to the United States for an official visit. The Polish pope accepted but said no to the American President for the rest. Carter had asked the IOR to stop laundering money from crime.

John Paul II turned a deaf ear and proclaimed, instead, his determination to bring the USSR down within ten years.

— The same way your President Kennedy set the target to go to the moon. My political target is that, and only that. If by chance the mafia's money was used to defeat the communist dictatorships, it wouldn't be used in such a bad way, he said bluntly.

Carter objected that the use of drugs wreaked havoc in the States. The pope retorted:

— If it's not provided by Europe, it will come from elsewhere, South America or Asia. The problem is drug consumption, not production. The solution is the same as with sexuality: abstinence.

He went on for a while.

— Mr. President, look what's just happened to my predecessor. The official story is natural death. But you know as well as I do, that's not the case. Those forces are too strong in Italy. I can't fight them upfront; I have to use them. Do you sail, Mr. President? One can't suppress the wind, but we can use it to go forward. I'm the first non-Italian pope since the 16th century. The Italian popes haven't managed to get rid of organized crime for half a millennium and it wasn't as widespread as today. How do you want a poor Polish pope to do it? Even with the help of the United States. You have Secret Services, the 6th fleet and missiles to protect yourselves. I have but the Swiss Guard and their halberds, in 15th century costumes!

Despite all your fantastic protection, they managed to kill President Kennedy. You can imagine the extreme physical weakness of a pope, head of a postage-stamp state! So please don't ask me to be stupidly heroic. I'm nothing and I think I'll have enough courage to face the risk. But not at a 99 to one risk of losing. On the other hand, I know all about the communist dictatorship. I can help to beat it. I have leverage there. Not in Sicily. If I tried, I would become a dead body. Fighting against the USSR also means a high risk of assassination. But in that fight, I have a chance to defeat them. It's four against one.

— Thank you, Your Holiness. Clear, logical but amoral. It's against the teaching of Christ to let money from crime be recycled under your very eyes. My Secret Services are clear about that. This is what's happening at the Vatican, and it has to stop.

— No lesson in morality, please Mr. President! What did you, the United States, do in 1943 and 1947? You woke the monster up again. Lucky Luciano, the Capo of all capi of the American mafia. You let him out of prison, you got rid of the devil in the States to send him to Naples . . . where he did more harm than before. And what has happened since? In Italy, your CIA backs up the most conservative forces, not to say neo-fascists; and it even tolerates the mafia to a certain extent. Same as us.

— I'm not like that, said Carter.

— I appreciate it, said the pope and respect you all the more for it. You have an ethical approach. Like the one to ban murders by your services during your mandate. It seems it's the first time an American President takes action against it. Carter was flabbergasted: how on earth could that damned Pole be aware of a State Secret like this one? But he didn't react. Nor contested it, nor denied it.

— Yes, but you only get an election every four years and can only stay in post a maximum of eight years, said John Paul II. What's that compared to the powers we are facing? Your successors will change the political game like a compass gone crazy; it leads you nowhere, whatever your good faith as actual president. I'm only 58 years old and I have a lifetime to reach the goal I have set myself. If God gives me enough time, I might succeed. You're younger than me, but even if you live a hundred years, which I hope for your sake, you will only be the President of the United States at the most until 1984. It's very little time to alter the course of the world. Above all with someone as determined as me!

And sure enough, two years later, Ronald Reagan replaced Jimmy Carter in the Oval Office. Reagan and John Paul II combined forces to bring down the USSR. In 1989, the Berlin Wall fell.

EPILOGUE

A phone rang. It was answered. At the other end, you could hear *"Why are you coughing"*?

That was all. It hangs up.

Exquisite Bodies

Michele Sindona, Roberto Calvi, Elio Cighi had people murdered who were investigating their cases.

In 1979 alone:

On March 29, 1979, in Milan, Judge Emilio Alessandrini was shot at a red light in his car by five men.

On March 20, 1979, in Rome, Mino Pecorelli, a member of the P2 lodge suspected of treason, was shot twice in the mouth while getting into his car.

On July 11, 1979, in Milan, the solicitor Giorgio Ambrosoli was assassinated in the street with four bullets.

On July 13, 1979, in Rome, Lieutenant-Colonel Antonio Varisco, head of the Roman security services, was killed in his car with his driver by four shots from a sawed-off shotgun.

On July 21, 1979, in Palermo, the investigator Boris Giuliano was shot six times in a crowded café. No one had seen anything.

In October 1979, in Milan, Enrico Cuccia, managing director of Mediobanca, a public investment bank, miraculously escaped a bomb attack.

On March 9, 1979, in Rome, Cardinal Jean-Marie Villot died of natural causes.

On June 17, 1982, in Milan, Graziella Corrocher, Roberto Calvi's secretary, "committed suicide" from the 4th floor window of the Banco Ambrosiano headquarters.

On June 18, 1982, Roberto Calvi "committed suicide" under a bridge in London.

On October 2, 1982, in Milan, Gino Dellacha, director of the Banco Ambrosiano, "committed suicide" from a window of the bank.

Michele Sindona was poisoned in his cell on March 22, 1986, while serving a sentence for the murder of Giorgio Ambrosoli.

Elio Cighi died a free man in his bed on November 14, 2014, at the age of 95.

Characters

- BERLINGUER Ernesto, leader of the ICP.
- BODROTTI Andrea, multiple times president of the Italian Council, leader of the DC representing his right wing, practicing Catholic, close to the popes Pius XII and Paul VI, suspected of being linked to the mafia. Says the Stainless.
- **BONASSOLI Aldo**, inventor, con artist. He lives in Lurano, Italy. First cousin of Albino Luciani and Nina Petri (Luciani). Cousin of Vittorio Petri.
- BURBON Paul, NSA Director. Four-year-old girl, Nelly. Married. 2 other children.
- CADALI Valentino, mafia boss in 1978. Notably murdered the Impastato father and son.
- CALVI Roberto, fascist, a banker, associated with the Vatican and the mafia, boss of Banco Ambrosiano. Mafia banker from 1974 to 1982, member of the lodge P2.
- CARTER Jimmy, President of the United States from 1976 to 1981.
- **CIGHI Elio**, fascist, financier, head of the lodge P2. Says the Puppeteer.
- DALO Gino, mafia boss in Palermo.
- DUBOIS Yves, abbot, Vatican diplomat at the UN, French intelligence agent.
- DUCE: title of the Italian dictator Benito Mussolini from 1921 to 1945.
- GAMBINO Carlo, American mafia boss after World War II.

- IMPASTATO Peppino, young Sicilian politician opposed to the mafia and murdered by it in 1978.
- JOHN XXIII, Angelo Roncalli, pope from 1958 to 1963.
- **John Paul I**: see Luciani.
- **JONES Nancy**, professor of mathematics and cryptography at the University of Rome, head of the NSA's Rome post. Companion of Vittorio Petri.
- **LOMBARDI Alessa**, a freelance journalist. Also published in the magazine Fendinebbia. Niece by alliance of American President Jimmy Carter.
- LUCIANO Lucky, godfather of American mafia bosses before and during World War II.
- **LUCIANI Albino**: Pope John Paul I, Giovanni Paolo I, Gianpaolo.
- MACCHI Pasquale, priest, secretary of Montini, then Paul VI from 1954 to 1978.
- MARCINKUS Paul, bishop, mafia associate, Vatican banker (I.O.R) from 1969 to 1989. Protected by Paul VI, then by John Paul II.
- **MONTINI Giovanni**, archbishop of Milan from 1954 to 1963, pope under the name of Paul VI from 1963 to 1978. Friend of Sindona.
- MUSSOLINI Benito, Italian dictator from 1921 to 1945.
- PACELLI Eugenio, Pope Pius XII from 1939 to 1958.
- **Paul VI**: see Montini.
- PETRI Ettore, married to Nina Petri (Luciani). Father of Vittorio Petri.
- PETRI Nina, born Nina Luciani, younger sister of Albino Luciani, mother of Vittorio Petri, wife of Ettore Petri, first cousin of Aldo Bonassoli.

- **PETRI Vittorio, IOR banker, nephew of Albino Luciani. His mother is Nina Petri. His father, Ettore Petri. Her friend is Nancy Jones. Cousin of Aldo Bonassoli.**
- PIUS XII, pope from 1939 to 1958. With fascist sympathy. Eugenio Pacelli.
- RONCALLI: see John XXIII.
- SINDONA Michele, mafia, mafia banker from 1957 to 1974. Member of the P2. Friend of Montini.
- WOJTYLA Karol, Cardinal of Krakow, then Pope John Paul II from 1978 to 2005.

Acronyms etc.

Ambrosiano Bank: fraudulent bankruptcy in 1982. CEO
Roberto Calvi

CD: Christian Democracy (leading political party in Italy)

CIA: Central Intelligence Agency (USA)

CIO: Chief Executive Officer

COSA NOSTRA: Sicilian mafia

CRYPTO AG: Swiss manufacturer of encryption machines
that are supposed to be tamper-proof and sold to more than
120 countries since 1955. The CIA installed a "back door"
there from the beginning.

CS: Credit Suisse (a bank)

CUPOLA: meeting of Sicilian mafia bosses

DOW JONES: US stock index

FENDINEBBIA: Italian magazine of reflection and analysis

ICP: Italian Communist Party

IOR: Istituto per le Opere di Religione, the Institute for the
Works of Religion, usually called the Vatican Bank

KGB: Komitet Gossoudarstvennoï Bezopasnosti (State
Security Committee of the former USSR)

NSA: National Security Agency (USA)

OCTOPUS: one of the nicknames of the mafia

P2: Propaganda Due, occult lodge of fascist tendency

SNB: Swiss National Bank (central bank)

USSR: Union of Soviet Socialist Republics (Soviet Union)

VATICAN BANK: common nickname of the IOR

ZUGZWANG: chess forced blow

Sources & Bibliography

• Benzinemag.net, mon sang retombera sur vous (my blood will fall on you), Cédric Vigneault, 6.6.2008.

• La difficile réforme des finances du Vatican (The difficult reform of the Vatican's finances), Antonino Galofaro, 6.1.2020.

• Le Monde, L'énorme scandale du Credit Suisse (The Huge Credit Suisse Scandal), F.R., May 17, 1977.

• Le Monde, Les responsables du scandale financier de Chiasso devant les tribunaux helvétiques (Those responsible for Chiasso's financial scandal before the Swiss courts), Jean-Claude Buhrer, May 29, 1979.

• In God's name, Investigation into the suspicious death of John Paul I, David Yallop, 1984, Bantam Books, new edition, 2011 Ed. New World.

• Le Temps, Crypto a espionné pour la Suisse, elle n'est pas la seule (Crypto spied for Switzerland, it is not the only one), Mehdi Atmani, Adrienne Fichter, Sylke Gruhnwald, November 11, 2020.

• Le Temps, Les grandes affaires économiques de la Suisse. Le scandale de Chiasso, ou l'histoire d'une banque dans la banque (The great economic affairs of Switzerland. The Chiasso scandal, or the story of a bank in the bank), Emannuel Garessus, July 31, 2008.

• Swissinfo, La grande leçon du scandale Texon (The great lesson of the Texon scandal), Gemma d'Urso, Lugano, 23.4.2002.

• Terrorism.net, Documents Brigades rouges : les communiqués de l'enlèvement d'Aldo Moro en 1978 (Documents Red Brigades: the statements of the kidnapping of Aldo Moro in 1978), Pierluigi Zoccatelli, March 16, 2003.
• Un système de corruption peu à peu révélé au grand jour au Vatican (A system of corruption gradually revealed in the Vatican), RTS, Valérie Dupont, 30.9.2020.
• Vatican - La cinquième loterie de charité du pape est lancée (Vatican - The fifth papal charity lottery is launched), Pierre Selas, 1.12.2017.

Wikipedia, The free encyclopedia: Aldo Moro, Money laundering, Red Brigades, Calogero Vizzini, Castel Gondolfo, Conclave of August 1978, Cosa Nostra, Crypto AG, Giuseppe Calò, Giorgio Ambrosoli, Giulio Andreotti, History of personal computers, Jean-Marie Villot, John Paul I, John Paul II, Lech Walesa, The Lead Years, Licio Gelli, Michele Sindona, Paul VI, Vatican Palace, Pasquale Macchi, Passeto di Borgo, Paul Marcinkus, Presidency of Jimmy Carter, Peter's Principle, Propaganda due, Pio La Torre, Cultural Revolution, Roberto Calvi, Scandal of Chiasso, Stefano Bontate, Strategy of tension, Assassination attempt of John Paul II, Conspiracy theories on the death of John Paul I, Tommaso Buscetta, Vito Ciancimino, War on drugs.

Thanks

My proofreaders, Kim, Marianne, Jérémie and Mathieu, made extremely relevant and decisive improvements to this story. I thank them warmly, as well as Géraldine and Francesca who translated the novel from French to English, and Anne, Wendy and Corey who proofread the English version partially or entirely.

Among the sources, I am particularly grateful to David Yallop and Wikipedia.

Table

CPSIA information can be obtained
at www.ICGtesting.com
Printed in the USA
LVHW051539210623
750377LV00003B/266

9 798374 590524